VOLUME THIRTEEN

ENCOUNTE
THE PHA

This was a killer's world. All the nocturnal predators prowled through it. He heard the low lunger moan of the hunting leopard as it tiptoed along tree branches. Distinctly he heard the cough of a tiger ... The noise was deafening and occasionally it was punctuated by the scream of a dying animal.

Suddenly all sound stopped as though a switch had been thrown. The silence was eerie, even more threatening, as though everything in the jungle were afraid of something more deadly than itself. Riggs' hand was stealing toward the rifle in the compartment on the side of the jeep.

From the darkness came a voice, a deep resonant voice...

Hermes Press

Published by Hermes Press, an imprint of Herman and Geer Communications, Inc.
Daniel Herman, Publisher
Troy Musguire, Production Manager
Eileen Sabrina Herman, Managing Editor
Alissa Fisher, Graphic Design
Kandice Hartner, Senior Editor
Benjamin Beers, Archivist

2100 Wilmington Road
Neshannock, Pennsylvania 16105
(724) 652-0511
www.HermesPress.com; info@hermespress.com

Cover image: Painting of The Phantom by George Wilson
Book design by Eileen Sabrina Herman
First printing, 2020

LCCN applied for: 0 1 2 3 4 5 6 7 8 9 10
ISBN 978-1-61345-192-2
OCR and text editing by H + G Media and Eileen Sabrina Herman
Proof reading by Eileen Sabrina Herman and Kandice Hartner

From Dan, Louise, Sabrina, Ruckus, and Noodle for D'zur and Mellow

Acknowledgements: This book would not be possible without the help, cooperation, patience, and kindness of many people. First and foremost in making this endeavor a reality are Ita Golzman and Frank Caruso at King Features. Thanks also to Pete Klaus and the late Ed Rhoades of "The Friends of the Phantom." Pete and Ed have provided us with resource material, contacts, information, and helpful insights into the strip and continue to be there when we have questions about the world of The Ghost Who Walks.

Editor's Note: There were several misspellings in the original text; those have been corrected with this reprint. However, the alternate spelling for the Singh pirates as Singg was kept to preserve the original format.

Printed in Canada

AUTHORS NOTE

Old friends of the PHANTOM adventure strip may be interested to know more about this series of novels with the general title, The Story of the Phantom.

All are based on my original stories. I wrote *They Story of the Phantom—The Ghost Who Walks, The Mysterious Ambassador, Killer's Town, The Vampires and the Witch*, and this book, *The Curse of the Two-Headed Bull.*

Basil Copper adapted *The Slave Market of Mucar*, and *The Scorpia Menace*. Frank S. Shawn adapted *The Veiled Lady, The Golden Circle, The Hydra Monster, The Mystery of the Sea Horse, The Goggle-Eyes Pirates*, and *The Swamp Rats*. Warren Shanahan adapted *The Island of Dogs*, and Carson Bingham adapted *The Assassins.*

Lee Falk
1974

The Story of THE PHANTOM and
The Island of Dogs

Lee Falk

CONTENTS

WITH THE PHANTOM, EVERYTHING IS POSSIBLE— EXCEPT BOREDOM

by
Francis Lacassin, Lecturer
The Sorbonne, Paris, France

When Lee Falk introduced into comic-strip format the imaginary and the fantastic with the figure of *Mandrake, The Magician*, it was apparent that he was contributing to what I describe to my students at the Sorbonne as "The Ninth Art." It was even more evident when he invented The Phantom, a figure who set the fashion for the masked and costumed Man of Justice,

On November 15, 1971, the oldest university in Europe, the Sorbonne, opened its doors to the comics. I was privileged to give, with the section of Graphic Arts, a weekly two-hour course in the History of the Aesthetics and Language of Comic Strips. Prior sessions had been devoted to the *Phantom*. The female students were drawn to the attractiveness and elegance of his figure; the men liked his masculinity and humor. To me, Lee Falk's stories—representing as they do the present-day *Thousand and One Nights*, fairy tales, *The Tales of the Knights of the Round Table*, etc.—adapt the epic poetry for the dreams and needs of an advanced and industrial civilization. For me the Phantom reincarnates Achilles, the valorous warrior of the Trojan War, and like a knight he wanders about the world in search of a crime to castigate or a wrong to right.

Lee Falk's art of storytelling is defined as much by the succinctness of the action, as by that of the dialogue. The text has not only a dry, terse quality, but also delicious humor. The humor shows itself in the action by the choice of daring ellipses: nothing remains but the strong points of the action. This allows the story to progress more rapidly and reduces the gestures of the hero to those which underlie his fantastic physical prowess. Falk gives the drama in a nutshell. A remarkable example is the resume done in four frames (in the comic strip) and placed at the beginning of each episode to recall the Phantom's origins. In four pictures, everything about the man is said, his romantic legend, his noble mission. Moreover, the new reader enters the fabulous world of Lee Falk, where nothing is real but everything is possible—except boredom.

Dressed in a soft hat and an overcoat with the collar upturned, the Phantom and his wolf, Devil, wander about the world, the cities of Europe, or, dressed in his eighteenth-century executioner's costume, he passes his time in the jungle. Wherever he is, he acts like a sorcerer of the fantastic. Under his touch, the real seems to crack and dreams well through.

A masked ball in the Latin Quarter appears. In the Phantom's eyes it is the rendezvous of a redoubtable secret society of women. The jungle vegetation becomes the jewel box in which are hidden lost cities, sleeping gods, vampire queens, tournaments worthy of the Olympic Games. The geography, the flowers, the animals in their turn undergo a magical change brought on by the hero. A savage continent borders the edge of the Deep Woods. It is protected by a praetorian guard, the pygmies. The Skull Cave contains the treasures of war and the archives of his ancestors. All this occurs on a mythical continent which is not exactly Africa nor exactly Asia, because the tigers and lions are friends.

The genius of Lee Falk is to have known how to create a new *Odyssey*, with all of its fantastic color, but what is even more surprising is that it would be believable in the familiar settings of the modern world. The Phantom acts with the audacity of Ulysses and also with the nobility of a knight-errant. In contrast to Ulysses, and similarly to Sir Lancelot, he moves about in the world of his own free will among his peers. Lee Falk has not only managed to combine epic poetry with fairy tales and the stories of chivalry, he has made of the Phantom, in a jungle spared by colonialism, an agent of political equilibrium and friendship between races. In giving his hero an eternal mission, Lee Falk has made him so real, so near, so believable that he has made of him a man of all times. He will outlive him as Ulysses has outlived Homer. But in contrast to Ulysses, his adventures will continue after his creator is gone, because his creator has made of him an indispensable figure endowed with a life of his own. This is a privilege of which the heroes of written word cannot partake; no one has been able to imitate Homer.

However, the comic strip is the victim of a fragile medium, the newspaper. Because of this, some adventures of *The Phantom* have been lost and live only in the memory of their readers. This memory is difficult to communicate to others. Lee Falk has, therefore, given a new dimension to *The Phantom* by making of him the hero of a series of novels, introducing his origins and his first adventures to those who did not know him before.

This is not his least important accomplishment, but the most significant in my opinion is this: —in presenting to us The Phantom, as a friend, Lee Falk has taught us to dream, which is something no school in the world can teach.

Francis Lacassin
June, 1972
Paris

PROLOGUE

How It All Began

*O*ver *four hundred years ago, a large British merchant ship was attacked by Singg pirates off the remote shores of Bangalla. The captain of the trading vessel was a famous seafarer who, in his youth, had served as cabin boy to Christopher Columbus on his first voyage to discover the New World. With the captain was his son, Kit, a strong young man who idolized his father and hoped to follow him as a seafarer. But the pirate attack was disastrous. In a furious battle, the entire crew of the merchant ship was killed and the ship sank in flames. The sole survivor was young Kit who, as he fell off the burning ship, saw his father killed by a pirate. Kit was washed ashore, half-dead. Friendly pygmies found him and nursed him to health.*

One day, walking on the beach, he found a dead pirate dressed in his fathers clothes. He realized this was the pirate who had killed his father. Grief-stricken, he waited until vultures had stripped the body clean. Then on the skull of his father's murderer, he swore an oath by firelight as the pygmies watched. "I swear to devote my life to the destruction of piracy, greed, cruelty, and injustice – and my sons and their sons shall follow me."

This was the Oath of the Skull that Kit and his descendants would live by. In time, the pygmies led him to their home in the Deep Woods in the center of the jungle, where he found a large cave with many rocky chambers. The mouth of the cave, a natural formation formed by the water and wind of centuries, was curiously like a skull. This became his home, the Skull Cave. He soon adopted a mask and a strange costume. He found that the mystery and fear this inspired helped him in his endless battle against world-wide piracy. For he and his sons who followed became known as the nemesis of pirates everywhere, a mysterious man whose face no one ever saw, whose name no one knew, who worked alone.

As the years passed, he fought injustice wherever he found it. The first Phantom and the sons who followed found their wives in many places. One married a reigning queen, one a princess, one a beautiful red-haired barmaid. But whether queen or commoner, all followed their men back to the Deep Woods to live the strange but happy life of the wife of the Phantom. And of all the world, only she, wife of the Phantom and their children, could see his face.

Generation after generation was conceived and born, grew to manhood, and assumed the tasks of the father before him. Each wore the mask and costume. Folk of the jungle and the city and sea began to whisper that there was a man who could not die, a Phantom, a Ghost Who Walks. For they thought the Phantom was always the same man. A boy who saw the Phantom would see him again fifty years after; and he seemed the same. And he would tell his son and his grandson; and then his son and grandson would see the Phantom fifty years after that. And he would seem the same. So the legend grew. The Man Who Cannot Die. The Ghost Who Walks. The Phantom.

The Phantom did not discourage this belief in his immortality. Always working alone against tremendous – sometimes almost impossible – odds, he found that the awe and fear the legend inspired was a great help in his endless battle against evil. Only his friends, the pygmies, knew the truth. To compensate for their tiny stature, the pygmies, mixed deadly poisons for use on their weapons in hunting or defending themselves. It was rare that they were forced to defend themselves. Their deadly poisons were known through the jungle, and they and their home, the Deep Woods, were dreaded and avoided. Another reason to stay away from the Deep Woods – it soon became known that this was a home of the Phantom, and none wished to trespass.

Through the ages, the Phantoms created several more homes, or hideouts, in various parts of the world. Near the Deep Woods was the Isle of Eden, where the Phantom taught all animals to live in peace. In the southwest desert of the New World, the Phantoms created an eyrie on a high, steep mesa that was thought by the Indians to be haunted by evil spirits and became known as "Walker's Table" – for the Ghost Who Walks. In Europe, deep in the crumbling cellars of ancient castle ruins, the Phantom had another hideout from which to strike against evildoers.

But the Skull Cave in the quiet of the Deep Woods remained the true home of the Phantom. Here, in a rocky chamber, he kept his chronicles, written records of all his adventures. Phantom after Phantom faithfully recorded their experiences in the large folio volumes. Another chamber contained the costumes of all the generations of Phantoms. Other chambers contained the vast treasures of the Phantom acquired over the centuries, used only in the endless battle against evil.

Thus twenty generations of Phantoms lived, fought, and died, usually violently, as they fulfilled their oath. Jungle folk, sea folk and city folk believed him the same man, the Man Who Cannot Die. Only the pygmies knew that always, a day would come when their great friend would die. Then, alone, a strong young son would carry his father to the burial crypt of his ancestors where all Phantoms rested. As the pygmies waited outside, the young man would emerge from the cave, wearing the mask, the costume, and the skull ring of the Phantom; his carefree, happy days as the Phantom's son were over. And the pygmies would chant their age-old chant, "The Phantom is dead. Long live the Phantom."

The story of the Island of Dogs is an adventure of the Phantom of our time—the twenty-first generation of his line. He has inherited the traditions and responsibilities created by four centuries of Phantom ancestors. One ancestor created the Jungle Patrol. Thus, today, our Phantom is the mysterious and unknown commander of this elite corps. In the jungle, he is known and loved as The Keeper of the Peace. On his right hand is the Skull Ring that leaves his mark— the Sign of the Skull—known and feared by evildoers everywhere. On his left hand—closer to the heart—is his "good mark" ring. Once given, the mark grants the lucky bearer protection by the Phantom, and it is equally known and respected. And to good people and criminals alike in the jungle, on the seven seas, and in the cities of the world he is the Phantom, the Ghost Who Walks, the Man Who Cannot Die.

Lee Falk
New York 1974

CHAPTER 1

The charter yacht, *Scotty's Pride*, moved smoothly through the sea, bow nodding into the easy swell, its powerful engines purring as comfortably as a milk-full kitten. The sun was warm, the breeze was cool, and it was as ideal and pleasant a day as any honeymoon couple could wish.

Phyllis and Jim Landon were on the flying bridge, seated in high turntable chairs fastened to the deck on each side of the veteran skipper-owner, Angus MacPherson, standing at the wheel. They were swaying with the yacht's motion, lulled to lassitude, eyeing the brightly lit waters in hypnotized fashion. Even Angus MacPherson's movements were lizard-slow; he'd glance at the compass, then shift the wheel a spoke's span, counteracting the tide and the torque of his propellers, holding to the magnetic course he had charted the night before.

Off to starboard, a height of land appeared on the horizon. Jim Landon blinked at it, pushing a shock of blond hair off his square forehead.

"Bangalla?" he queried.

"Aye." The single-word answer came out in a puff of smoke from the curved pipe that seemed to hang permanently from the skipper's lips. The pipe was more permanent than his teeth, he occasionally remarked.

Phyllis, the beautiful brunette bride, sat up straighter in her chair, and pointed toward the land. "Isn't that what they used to call Skull Peak?"

"They still do," MacPherson answered in his rich Scottish burr, "but you'll notice there's no resemblance to a skull."

Jim Landon studied it. "I can see where once it might have looked like a skull. But growing vegetation—perhaps a rockfall."

MacPherson nodded and turned the wheel another spoke. Speculation and theory didn't interest him. He was a practical man.

Phyllis and Jim were fascinated by the jutting rock rising mysteriously out of the sea, dwarfing everything around it, giant trees growing on it appearing no bigger than grass. Phyllis, wearing a bathing suit, unconsciously pulled her cotton twill jacket tighter over her bare shoulders, protecting them from the sun. It was an unthinking gesture. Her fair skin had acquired a tan on the voyage.

She said, "Perhaps that is where all the stories of the Phantom originated."

The skipper scratched the back of his weathered neck with his pipe stem. "Oh, aye. Stories. That's all they be."

"Yet," Jim turned to him, "I've seen men with a skull mark on their jaws. Those men were shunned, avoided as though they were carriers of evil. I've seen them in European cities, although I suspect most men bearing the skull mark try to hide in obscure places. But those I've seen—a check of their available records proves you do well to avoid them."

MacPherson nodded. "I've also seen men with the skull mark. All you say is true. Once I thought it was an initiation symbol, they belonged to a brotherhood of crime you might say. Now I believe they were caught committing a crime and were branded for their efforts by some sort of . . . uh," he searched for the proper words, "a society that believes in good. A group that is anti-criminal, anti-evil."

Jim laughed. "That sounds like the Jungle Patrol."

"This is Jungle Patrol country, right enough. They're headquartered in Mawitaan. We'll be there tomorrow past noon . . . providing the weather holds," he added with his usual caution.

Phyllis looked back at the headland, and said regretfully, "Then there is no Phantom?"

MacPherson's eyes were in a perpetual squint from staring into sunlit waters. He checked his compass, turned the wheel, fractionally, glanced at Dongalo, and his crew. Dongalo was a true seaman, one of the Mori fisherfolk, and had the interminable patience of his people. Now he was sprawled motionless with his head on a coil of line. But let there be a hiccup in the engines, or a slight change in the roll of the ship to show the waters were shallowing, and he was up instantly. Whether he was asleep or awake was debatable. That he was alert was certain.

MacPherson tried to answer with care Phyllis Landon's question: Then there is no Phantom? "Let me put it this way," his Scottish burr was becoming more pronounced, "I hae lived my Biblical three score and ten, and a bit more. I'm in reasonable good health. I possess most of my faculties, and I've seen many strange things there's nae explaining. I believe because I hae seen them, and I'm a man with a good deal of skepticism."

"You believe the skull marks on the jaw?" Jim interrupted.

"Aye. I said I hae seen them."

"The few criminals arrested who were bearing the skull mark had those marks subjected to scientific analysis. I should say the police did it, not the criminals. The marks are permanent, correct?"

"So I've heard."

"The examining scientists are baffled. They say the marks are applied with tremendous force, much more than one man could exert, even a professional boxer. Yet each of the criminals—every one of them—said they were struck on the jaw by the Phantom. They saw the Phantom."

"Or thought they saw the Phantom. I dare say they were in a bit of a shock at the time. Being caught red-handed at doing whatever they were doing."

Jim, usually good-natured, was very intent now. "Shock and trauma were taken into account. These criminals were questioned separately. We asked them to give descriptions to a police artist. In every case, the details were the same."

Angus had a slight smile on his lips. "Perchance would these descriptions also match those of a crime-fighter in Europe, and another in the United States?"

Jim was a bit disgruntled. "Well . . . yes."

"So, laddie," MacPherson exhaled a column of smoke, "we come back to the group theory again. No one man is strong enough to leave the mark of the Phantom. Your own scientists state that. You, yourself, admit the Phantom is on three continents. The rest is legend, laddie, only legend."

The old skipper turned to Phyllis. "There you have it, bonny lass. It's all a romantic story. Show me a man who's four hundred years old, who's strong, fit, active. Show me a Man Who Cannot Die. Show me a man who can do more than mortal man. Then I'll believe in the Phantom."

"The Phantom lives." Dongalo was standing below the flying bridge, staring up at them. "The Phantom is," he assured them, and stalked to the bow.

Jim laughed. "There's your answer for you, Mr. MacPherson."

"Nay," Angus shook his head. "That's no answer. That's faith."

"Then you think the Jungle Patrol implants the skull mark?"

"I would say no to that, too. I never heard of the skull mark in connection with them."

"Then who does it?"

"A group. A society." He nodded at the Bangalla coast. "There's a lot of jungle that's barely explored. A lot behind it few men have seen. I cannot guess at all the wonders of the world."

"A group," Jim mused, then added, "it would have to be a worldwide group, an international society."

"Then there is no Phantom?" Phyllis's tone plainly expressed her regret.

"The facts speak against it," Angus MacPherson said kindly.

"He is the Ghost Who Walks," Dongalo stated from the bow. "The Phantom lives."

CHAPTER 2

They anchored overnight. They were approaching shoal waters, largely uncharted, too dangerous to run in the dark. All the warning lights were much farther out to sea, where the oceangoing vessels could see them and steer clear. This close to Bangalla, coast lights were not considered necessary and the expense not warranted.

The next morning Skipper MacPherson was navigating the channel. The Landons came from below, from the galley where their huge breakfasts had been prepared by Dongalo, who proudly exhibited another of his skills. They took their usual seats on the flying bridge. Angus MacPherson was puffing the initial pipe of the day.

Phyllis saw it first, demonstrating her extraordinary eyesight. "Is that an island?" she called attention to what appeared as a low cloud on the horizon.

"It could be," MacPherson nodded. "There is one at that approximate position."

"What is it called?"

"The Island of Dogs."

"How peculiar. Why is it named that? Shaped like a dog?"

"No, nothing of the kind," Angus turned the wheel and started the story.

Many generations ago, the natives always captured stray dogs, not wanting them to turn wild and become yet another menace in the hostile jungle. Because these men killed only for food, they had to dispose of the dogs humanely; therefore, they took them out to the nameless island and turned them free. Unwittingly, they were creating a horror, a sort of Frankenstein monster.

Beyond the beach, the island was largely barren rock, a few palm trees here and there struggling for survival. There was no source of fresh water; the rains were not frequent and the pools collecting in natural hollows tended to evaporate quickly. This lack of water was one of the basic causes for what happened later. The other was lack of food.

A man could have survived on the Island of Dogs, as it came to be known among the natives. He could have found a method of conserving water. The sea would have fed him.

The dogs, with limited intelligence, completely lacking toolmaking abilities, had little chance for survival. The first few abandoned on the island nearly starved before they learned to eat crustaceans down near the beach. Seaweed added to their diet. With this heavy intake of salt, the first battles occurred over water. Water was life, so these were battles to the death. There were few survivors; rangy muscular dogs, tough-jawed, sharp-fanged, and smart. There was water and food enough for these few, and there was peace among them.

Then canoeloads of new dogs were dumped onto the island. In general, they were better fed and in much better physical condition than the survivors of the first war, but they lacked the others' ruthless battle conditioning. As soon as the second group went to look for drinking water, they met the gaunt survivors.

Again, there were snarling, raging battles in which bodies rolled on sand and rock, and each ended with only one survivor. Those who had lived through the first war—and the second—had not eaten well in a long time; therefore, they devoured the dead, and were attacked by other starving dogs during their act of cannibalism.

Packs formed and dissolved. Allegiances changed as leaders fought and died. There was internecine warfare among the groups to determine the pecking order, and the savage battles always ended in death, for the strong devoured the weak. Whenever two packs met, the battle began immediately without any of the preliminaries usual to canines. Numbers diminished daily, hourly. Through the night, the pack battles raged and howls of defiance were raised to the moon.

It was inevitable that only a few would be left, limping, torn, craftier for having lived through such terror. There were no alliances here, no pack formation for self-protection. These survivors, barely self-sufficient, trusted no one, and there was a kind of peace founded upon fear.

Again, a load of dogs was dumped on the island and again the horror began. Again there were only a few who lived, and the cycle was repeated time and time again.

Generations of men had been bringing stray dogs to the Island of Dogs and it became something of a ritual. These men had heard on the wind the terrible baying and the vicious fighting, and while they would never have tolerated such cruelty on the mainland, habit had attained a religious significance, and now they believed stray dogs "belonged" to the island; it was their duty to bring them there.

They were not ignorant men, nor were they unkind. It was just that their only means of interpreting the supernatural was through natural means. Inevitably they were enlightened.

A number of canoes brought over yet another load of strays who shivered and yipped fearfully as they sensed what awaited them on this terrible island. Shark fins circled close, for often the sharks fed when fighting dogs came rolling over the cliffs still snapping at each other. None of the men liked this trip either, but it was important it be made, or more significantly, they believed it was important.

The moment the outriggers touched shore, the fear-filled dogs jumped to the beach and raced away to the left. The natives were astonished. This action was most peculiar. Usually they had to pull the strays out, actually desert them.

The explanation for the strange behavior soon became apparent.

From out of the rocks on the right, nightmares appeared. Gaunt dogs, hollow-ribbed, lean-flanked, sharp-fanged, slavering, eyes glowing red with insanity. They moved slowly and purposefully, one step at a time. To them, these humans were meat, food. They had lost all fear of men, all feelings of comradeship. Now they stalked them as prey.

The natives panicked at the sight of these dogs who were truly mad. Quickly they shoved their outriggers into the waters, and jumped aboard. And the mad dogs charged after them, howling eagerly, even leaping into the water in an attempt to climb into the canoes. The men paddled furiously, not attempting the rhythmic stroke they always used but digging independently for speed and more speed. The hounds, with the single-mindedness of insanity, strained in the water to catch them.

Then triangular fins cut in towards the dogs. The shovel noses of sharks appeared. Slitted mouths opened revealing needlepointed teeth. The torpedo-shaped bodies lunged in, twisted. There were yelps of astonishment and pain, then the canines were jerked under the waves.

The natives kept paddling, gradually gaining the rhythmic stroke that propelled them for endless miles of voyaging. They never looked back at the carnage in the sea. That was the last time dogs were brought to the Island of Dogs.

But it was not the end of the mindless, furious survival battles. No one was present to record events; conjecture must take the place of observation.

Eventually there would be one lone survivor, most likely weak and bleeding from wounds. When he died, the tragic and bloody history of the Island of Dogs would come to an end.

Scotty's Pride was close enough to the island now for them to see the beach. Phyllis asked, "And nothing else has been on the island since then?"

"Aye," Skipper MacPherson nodded. "Nothing in the memory of man. It's the lack of water, you see."

Phyllis looked at her new husband. "Oh, Jim, it's such a beautiful beach. We can picnic there."

Jim was puzzled. "MacPherson said something about sharks."

The decision had been shifted to Angus. His first concern was his passengers' safety. Then he took into account the time factor; so long as they entered Mawitaan before dark, they'd be on a reasonable schedule.

"There's no danger from sharks if you stay in shallow water. Dongalo can prepare a picnic basket, then take you in the tender."

"I'll take her in," Jim answered quickly, the thrill of exploration on him. He too, like Phyllis, was now eager to explore the island where such grisly events had occurred.

It was as though Angus MacPherson could read their minds—or perhaps he remembered how it was to be young. "I'd stay away from the cliffs. And dinna go too far inland. As I recall, it's shaped like a bowl and cannot be seen from the sea. Get in trouble there and it'll take time to fetch you."

"We'll be all right," Jim assured him.

Phyllis sat in the bow while Jim handled the small outboard engine propelling the little rowboat. Besides the picnic basket, their preparations included what they considered suitable clothing. Phyllis wore a bathing suit, a jacket over her shoulders, a bandanna to keep her wavy hair out of her eyes, and bathing slippers; Jim wore only a turtleneck sweater over his bathing trunks, and had on deck shoes to protect his feet from sharp rocks.

He beached the boat skillfully. Phyllis took the picnic basket; he dropped a mushroom anchor into the soft sand to hold the boat against the tide. Overhead the seagulls squabbled eternally about their food from the sea.

"Well," Phyllis put down the basket halfway up the beach and with hands on hips looked around. "Well, this place certainly does seem deserted. No empty beer cans or bottles."

Jim smiled grimly at Phyllis's mention of the marks of civilization—or, rather, at the lack of them here. He pointed to a line of bushes just beyond the beach, growing in sere earth, thrusting bayonet leaves as high as eight or ten feet.

"Let's see what's beyond them. There seems to be a passage through."

They walked up the beach, negotiating carefully through the cutting spikes of the bushes, then stood stock-still, staring.

Some thirty or forty yards away a high chain link fence, and on top of it, increasing its height, were three strands of barbed wire.

"But the island is deserted," Jim muttered, frowning.

"I guess it's not." Phyllis started running. She turned her head, teeth sparkling, eyes laughing. "Come on, slowpoke, I'll race you to it."

Jim was after her immediately. Phyllis was reaching out for the fence, trying to touch it first. Jim was reaching to grab her by the waist, throw her in the air and catch her as she came down. A seagull swooped over their heads and the bird was the first to the fence.

It came in to land on the top strand, feet forward, wings outstretched, braking. As the claws touched the barbed wire, one fluttering wing touched one of the galvanized posts that supported the fence every twelve feet.

There was a zapping-cracking sound, a bright flash like miniature lightning. The gull was thrown backwards as if from a catapult, landing on its back, wings limp, one leg cruelly twisted, a slight tendril of smoke rising over its inert body.

Phyllis and Jim stopped in their tracks. Jim got down on one knee, touched the bird's body. It was as warm as if it had been cooked with its feathers on.

Jim looked up, forehead creased. Phyllis took a trembling hand away from her mouth. "What . . . what happened?"

"Dead . . . hot . . . the fence! It must be electrified."

She stepped back, physically repelled. "I . . . I almost touched it!" she was aghast. Then she pointed with quivering finger. "Look! Look!"

Jim read. The sign said:

PRIVATE PROPERTY
KEEP OFF
TRESPASSERS
WILL BE SHOT

He mused, "The island isn't entirely deserted. Someone put up the fence. Someone generates the electricity."

"I don't like this place." Phyllis put her arms through the sleeves of the jacket. "Let's leave."

"You wait at the boat. I'm going to follow the fence line. Maybe I can see what's so valuable that they have to protect it with an electric fence."

"Are you crazy?" Phyllis exclaimed. "I'm coming with you. I'm not going to wait alone at the boat."

Jim grinned. "Okay. We'll try going this way." Approximately every hundred feet there was another sign warning that this was private property and trespassers would be shot. Nowhere, Jim noted grimly, was there a sign that the fence was electrified. It was as if they wanted people to blunder against the chain links, eliminate them as nuisances.

But who would put up such a fence? And why? The Island of Dogs was supposedly deserted due to lack of water, and while a water problem could be overcome by a desalinization plant or possibly wells, there was still the fact the island was out of the way, and surrounded by shoals and reefs.

An amplified voice blared, pounding at their ears, startling them. "Get off the island. Read the sign. You've been warned."

Jim's head was up. His eyes raced back and forth. "A bull horn. They can see us. We should be able to see them."

"Private property," the bullhorn roared. "Get out Last warning."

"That answers one question," Jim said. "The island's not deserted."

"Let's go," Phyllis's voice quavered.

Jim stood his ground and shouted, "Who are you? Show yourself." He was angry from frustration. The fence was not only to keep people out, but obviously was designed to injure or kill.

Jim got an answer. A rifle cracked and a bullet hissed past their heads. His anger turned to fury.

"What the ... ? How dare . . . ? I'll. . ."

The rifle banged again. Dust and dirt splattered over their feet, it was that close. Instinctively they jumped back. Again the hidden rifle went off, and the bullet whistled between them, a dangerous warning that the next bullet would be aimed at them. They turned and ran.

Bullets chased them all the way down the beach, and the rifle stopped firing only when they launched the boat and started the motor.

CHAPTER 3

There was an official reception at the residence of the Lord Mayor of Mawitaan, Ito Togando. Among the honored guests were Police Chief Togando; General Togando; Chief Justice Togando; Okan Togando, whose only title was Chairman of the Bangalla Bank, and Gando Togando, publisher of the daily newspaper, who had no title at all but was treated with a curious amount of respect by the Togando family. Also present were Colonel Randolph Weeks of the Jungle Patrol, and foreign dignitaries who represented nations with trading interests in Mawitaan.

The giant black Police Chief Togando was chatting with Colonel Weeks. They had mutual interest in maintaining law and order in, respectively, the port city of Mawitaan, and the jungle area surrounding. Both had found they could transact more business and exchange more productive ideas at their informal sessions than they could at regular monthly meetings, where they were surrounded by aides who insisted on strict protocol and were so stuffy about enforcing rules that nothing worthwhile could be accomplished in the limited time left after all the formalities had been observed.

Jim and Phyllis Landon had had letters of introduction to both Police Chief Togando and Colonel Weeks, and had turned them over to the port officials. Naturally they hadn't reached the hands of the persons they were addressed to. The canny Angus MacPherson, however, knew where the real power was, and brought them to the office of Gando Togando, publisher of the *Mawitaan Daily*, an influential newspaper read up and down the Bangalla coast and far beyond.

Eyes half-lidded, hands folded under chin, Gando listened to their tale with Buddha-like passivity, occasionally nodding to encourage one or the other if they paused.

When they were finished, Jim said, "You don't believe us, do you?"

"My dear sir and madam," Gando spread his hands wide. "I certainly think your story calls for investigation, although I, myself, do not possess the resources. The hallmark of a good reporter is to get other people to perform their official functions, and then write about what they accomplish. That, I think, is called news." He tilted his chair back. The single little action, typical of so many men who spend long hours at a desk, revealed his humanness to the Landons, and inspired confidence in them as to his abilities as an editor.

"I think," he said, "some letters of introduction were mentioned?"

"Perhaps by Mr. MacPherson, not by us," Jim answered,

"Ah, yes. Do you have them with you?"

"No. We turned them over to the authorities who boarded Mr. MacPherson's boat. They assured us they would be delivered to Police Chief Togando and Colonel Weeks."

"Oh, they will, they will. In a week or two. We are like all civilized nations, cursed with bureaucrats who are impressed with their own importance and are always trying to prove it. I remember one time in France . . . but my experiences hardly interest you." He spun in his chair, opened the desk drawer, took out two large white squares of cardboard. "I'm sure if Police Chief Togando and Colonel Weeks knew you were here in Mawitaan, they would request your presence at the official reception this evening. In their names, I invite you."

"But, I . . . we . . ." Jim began.

"If it's a matter of dress, I can recommend a really excellent seamstress for Mrs. Landon. An aunt of mine, in fact. And as for a tailor . . ." he looked at Jim.

Jim smiled. "Another Togando?"

Gando smiled in return. "Yes, we do seem numerous, but that is because our forebears were paramount chiefs. Their dignity demanded they have many wives, several hundred in one case. Naturally the chief's children were the best-educated, therefore, the Togandos were self-perpetuating. You must remind me to tell you of some of our more famous ancestors. Another time, of course.

Meanwhile, you'll have preparations to make for this evening."

They still seemed doubtful, so Gando tried to be tactful. "My aunt . . . and my uncle, the tailor . . . will be glad to establish a charge account."

"No, no," Phyllis waved the suggestion aside. "We have clothes we hope will be suitable for the occasion. But won't we be imposing? I ·mean we don't even know the Lord Mayor."

Gando understood the English mind. "My dear friends," he spread his arms expansively, "be my guests."

"Oh, in that case," Jim nodded agreement.

At the reception, Gando waited till Police Chief Togando and Colonel Weeks separated themselves from the crowd —as he knew they would—then he stalked them cleverly, sort of backing towards them. He showed surprise that they were standing where he could bump into them, then asked innocently, "Have you seen Mr. MacPherson?"

Colonel Weeks nodded his leonine head. "Scotty was here, disturbed about something. Wanted to talk to me. Then he saw you enter with that young couple and wandered off. Said something about needing a drink after what he had been through."

Chief Togando smiled hugely. "When Scotty's on shore, he doesn't need much of an excuse for having a drink."

"Perhaps," Gando suggested, "he had a decent reason this time."

Colonel Weeks looked sharply at him. He knew Gando to be a clever man who dug after truth with many shovels. Calmly, Gando turned and beckoned to the couple he had entered with.

As they approached, he explained the reason for their presence. "The people who chartered Scotty's yacht. I'd like you to meet them. I think they'll tell you what Scotty was upset about."

He introduced them, and Colonel Weeks was plainly puzzled. "Landon? Jim Landon? Some time ago I received a signal from an old schoolmate of mine, Brian Landon, saying his son might be coming by this way."

"Yes, sir, he's my father."

"Well, well! Can't say you're a chip; much larger edition. How is the old boy? Still Chief Inspector of the Murder Squad?"

"No, sir. Superintendent now."

"Excellent. Won't be long before he's Commissioner. And this beautiful girl is your wife, eh. Don't know how you young fellows do it. Obviously she's much too good for you."

Phyllis quickly identified the line of banter this bluff-appearing man was using, and joined in a temporary alliance with him. "I've been telling him that for quite some time," she beamed. "There was nothing impulsive about our courtship. He pursued and pursued. Finally I consented. A girl has to get married some time!" she shrugged.

"Yes," Colonel Weeks growled through a smoke cloud from his battered old briar, "but surely you could have done better."

"Very poor pickings this year. Best of a bad lot."

"Nonsense. Have a barracks full of handsomer chaps. More talented too."

"He's got you there, Phyllis," Jim laughed. "The Jungle Patrol is the elite of the elite."

"Maybe you could still take him off my hands," Phyllis suggested.

"Sorry," Colonel Weeks shook the mane on his head. "Too late now. Married. Against the rules. Might have used him once. I recall a James Landon who was quite a fair miler at Oxford. Might have been a great one if he wasn't taking honors."

Jim laughed again, put his arm around Phyllis and squeezed her shoulders. The smile he got in return revealed the warmth of her personality. "I'm glad I never did apply. Couldn't have stood the rejection."

Phyllis said to the Colonel, "Even if you had thrown him back, I guess I would have kept him."

Gando had a subtle mind, especially when seeking a front-page story. What the Landons had given him so far wasn't deserving even of a squib, but with the instincts of a good reporter he sensed something bigger. All it would take to develop was a little pushing and prodding of the proper authorities. He shut off the flow of reminiscences by saying, "Perhaps the Landons will tell you something of their recent adventures."

"Oh, yes." Jim suddenly became very serious. "Who lives on the Island of Dogs?"

"No one," Colonel Weeks answered, concerned at the quick change in the Landons' mood. "It's uninhabitable. No water."

"Water or not, it's growing an electric fence right now . . . signs that say trespassers will be shot . . . and a rifleman who put a number of bullets very close to us."

Police Chief Togando, bored with the conversation, was eyeing the crowd with the suspicious yet understanding eyes of a good cop. Now he turned his bulk around.

Both he and Colonel Weeks exclaimed, "What!" Since one was a baritone and the other was a bass, the music stopped and all the guests stared. Togando shifted again to hide the young couple from public view. "Find out more, Randolph," he asked the Chief Officer of the Jungle Patrol.

Colonel Weeks was clamping his teeth on his pipe. "An electric fence," he muttered. "Shot at! You're sure of this?"

"Of course we are," Phyllis protested. "I was almost frightened out of my bikini."

Police Chief Togando stopped a waiter. "Mr. MacPherson is probably at the bar. Would you extend our compliments, ask him to stop by here a moment."

"Don't you believe us?" Phyllis was indignant.

Chief Togando's bass voice was, among other things, a musical instrument that could soothe. "It isn't a matter of disbelief, ma'am. It's a matter of collecting all the available facts in order—as a colleague of mine once said, 'to avoid making a damn fool out of yourself.' That was my instructor at Scotland Yard. A Brian Landon, in point of fact."

Angus MacPherson came across the room with the rolling gait of a sailor. He was dressed respectably in a spotless white suit made for a larger man, and from the way he twitched his nose as he inhaled deeply, it was obvious he had had more than a few nips "to steady his nerves."

"Scotty," Colonel Weeks began, "did you see these young people being shot at?"

"Aye. I heard the first shot, put my glasses on the beach. Must have been an automatic rifle concealed in the rocks above. Chased this lass and lad right down the beach, he did, and wasn't missing by much. A bad ricochet could have wounded them—or worse. I can tell ye I didna spare my engines getting out of there or getting here. Now if you'll excuse me my nerves are in a very sorry state and need just a touch more soothing."

They watched him walk away. Colonel Weeks clapped Jim Landon on the shoulder. "I can promise you we'll investigate! A man who uses a weapon to scare off people will hear something about it."

"Thank you, Colonel," Jim said. "If we hadn't been so scared, probably we'd have let it pass."

"Nonsense, my boy. You did the right thing. I'll send your father a copy of the report."

"Gando," Police Chief Togando made a pointed suggestion "aren't you going to introduce the Landons to the rest of our family and guests?"

Gando smiled. The story was developing. The proper authorities had been pushed. Now he could afford to wait.

After they were alone, Colonel Weeks said, "Well, old friend, any help I can supply, just let me know."

"Help me!" Togando was startled. "Randolph, my jurisdiction

goes barely beyond the port."

"My jurisdiction doesn't go that far out to sea," Colonel Weeks protested.

Chief Togando rubbed his round chin with a huge hand. "We have a problem, my friend. A crime has been committed."

"Yes," Randolph Weeks bit down on his pipe stem. "And who's going to solve it?"

The Phantom sat on the Skull Throne, resting. Of all the proud titles he bore—the Ghost Who Walks, Man Who Cannot Die—he was proudest of the title, Keeper of the Peace. Ages ago, the First Phantom had decided there would be peace in the jungle. Tribes traditionally warred on each other in eons-old arguments over land boundaries, water rights, hunting grounds. There were also cannibal tribes, and aggressive tribes who sought to extend their domains and their numbers by marked and bloody conquest.

It took generations of Phantoms to bring peace, and even then disruptive elements were constantly arguing for war, or actually waging war. However, the long line of Phantoms fought these warmongers, exerted all of the might of their power against aggressors. Under the rigorous law of Darwinian Selection, those who preached war and waged war did not live to breed, and perpetuate their evil. It was an old jungle saying that those who turned their backs on the Phantom discovered they faced Death. Gradually the numbers of those who violated law and order were diminished in the same manner a good gardener weeds his plot. It was a long, seemingly endless process, but help came from the tribes as they, in turn, found great benefits deriving from the Phantom's Peace. They, too, fought those who would break the peace.

The Phantom, like many astute observers, had noticed that after all great wars there were protracted peace negotiations between victors and conquered. The defeated, of course, had lost everything and the victors had won nothing, therefore, it would have been more beneficial to both if they had settled their differences at the conference table before they started fighting each other. What did it take to support a small group of diplomats compared to supporting a vast army with all its weapons? Victorious nations had been economically bankrupted by the winning of a war.

Therefore, the Phantom's Peace was established and the Phantom's Laws laid down. An animal was killed for food, never for pleasure. Since criminals always existed, and there were those who were criminally insane through no fault of their own, a man had the right and duty to protect his property, to save his life, and the lives of his family before his own. There would be no war. Those who traded with each other, those who shared a common boundary, would send a delegation to each other and all differences that had arisen would be discussed. If no agreement could be reached, then the chief of a third tribe—a neutral tribe not involved in the argument—would judge and weigh the merits of each argument and give his decision, and if still there was an unsatisfied party, then the difficulty would be brought before the Skull Throne, and woe to the obstinate, the obdurate, the hardhearted. If there were no arguments between neighboring or trading tribes, a delegation would still be sent as a symbol of the enduring Peace, and one member of that delegation would carry a shield bearing the Phantom's good sign, the sign that came from the ring on his left hand (closest to his heart), and the delegation would be honored, and any little matters that irked an individual would be brought before the delegation, and the delegation would be generous in their judgment.

So Peace came to the jungle and had existed longer than the memory of a grandfather's grandfather. All knew the Phantom would emerge from the mysterious Skull Cave if his Laws were broken, and there was a feeling of security in that. There was always a criminal element, a group or an individual who wanted power and luxury without working for it; there were faraway tribes well beyond the Deep Woods who sometimes came raiding and fell on the People of the Peace, and there were terrifying rumors of cannibal tribes. The People of the Peace had decided long ago that it was good the Phantom sat in the Skull Cave and watched all, and extended his protection to those who kept the Laws.

At approximately the same time the Landons were driven from the Island of Dogs, the Llongo peace delegation was leaving the Mori fisherfolk in a borrowed canoe. They had come by land bearing the Peace Shield, marching for days around the great Bight of Bangalla, and now the Mori, ever generous, were lending them an outrigger whereby they could cut across the Bight and reduce the time spent on the arduous journey home.

It was a joyous farewell. The Llongo and the Mori had traded peacefully for decades; lumber, metal and meat for the staple dried fish, and mile-long hunting nets strong enough to hold a herd of buffalo, made by craftsmen skilled in the knotting of gossamer nets so fine they could catch the little killie-like fish that were considered a delicacy. The peace talks had been, as usual, a time of celebration. The few individuals who felt they deserved more for their work were treated with the traditional openhandedness of the Llongo—so much so that in some extreme cases the individual was shamed into heaping gifts on the delegation to take back to the Llongo people.

As the Llongo paddled away into Bangalla Bay, the shouts of "come back soon" were genuine and heartfelt. Then the land fell out of sight as the strong arms of the Llongo drove the outrigger. These jungle-bred men knew little of canoeing, believed it was simply a matter of going in a straight line from one point to another. Even though they had been told by the Mori that the sea was unrelentingly cruel to those who disdained its ways, they looked upon the water with something akin to contempt—it was not one of the implacable elements they knew.

Their ignorance was immediately punished. They were caught in a wicked current, a mighty flow that surged off the Bangalla coast with so much power that even the ocean liners avoided it. The Llongo discovered that the point of land they were aiming for on the far shore was growing smaller instead of larger. Batu, the helmsman, shouted orders to increase the number of strokes. The Llongo sweated and still their goal receded. Batu called for more power. The paddlers strained, muscles standing out in ridges, and they learned that canoeing as practiced by the Mori was neither a sport nor a pleasure but a skilled occupation. They learned that muscles trained in the jungle were not necessarily those used on the sea. They hurt because they fought the current instead of using it as the Mori would have done. Their pain gave them knowledge.

Batu saw the Island of Dogs, and although he had heard of its reputation, he steered for it lest he and his men be swept out to sea. They needed rest, and he needed time to study the situation. An hour would do for both.

As soon as they entered the shoal waters, they were out of the inexorable force of the current. They could feel the giant grip leave them and they panted with exhaustion, slapping at the water more than paddling.

Batu exhorted them, "Just a little further. All together now. Stroke! Stroke!"

They picked up the rhythm with limp arms, raw palms, strained backs. But as long as there was a place where they could set their feet on land, they were willing, and their eagerness carried them to the beach of the Island of Dogs.

It was instinctive for them to pick up their spears and shields before thinking of rest. Jungle-bred, they were as cautious as the cats that stalked them. Indeed, they still wore the headdress that was symbolic of the manes of the lions they had once hunted as a threat to their survival— this, of course, before Phantom's Law. Now, as they leaned on their spears and their breathing returned to normal, they heard a tremendous blast of sound.

"Get off. This is a private island."

Instantly shields were up and spears back in the defense position.

"Who speaks?" Batu asked. "A giant?"

"Never have I heard a voice of such power," Tuga admitted. "It must be a giant."

"Where is he?"

They shifted uneasily, moving into a half-circle, shields still up.

"Get off the island."

"What does he say?" Mala wanted to know.

Bam shook his head, the flowing blond mane whispering. "Not Llongo," he stated the obvious. "Not Mori. Not Wambesi. No language I know."

"The Mori," Tuga made a point, "said this island was not inhabited by men. Could a giant have taken up residence here?"

"You are warned. Leave the island."

Mala snorted his disdain. "Must be a shy giant. He doesn't show himself."

Mala spoke for the rest of the Llongo warriors. From childhood, they had been trained to face the dangers of the jungle. They knew the charge of the mad elephant, the spring of the leopard, the stampede of two-ton buffalo, the hooking swing of a rhino's horn, and they had survived them all. They were warrior men, not children to be frightened by a loud noise.

They were moving in closer now, curious, even eager to see the giant. When they came upon the fence, they stopped to study it. Kantara, ever courageous, took a few steps forward and used an underhand thrust to put his spear point in a warning sign.

"What does this say?"

Batu eyed it, stirring up his memory. "Hmmm. The characters look like those Phantom sometimes uses. But I cannot read them."

"Well," Mala stepped further forward, "perhaps this fence is to keep the giant in, perhaps it is to keep us out. In either case I think we'll have a story to tell Phantom when he visits us."

"Last warning. Get out of here."

Mala stabbed with his spear, trying to cut through the chain link. There was that lightning flash, that snapping sound as of a tree cracking in a hurricane, and Mala was thrown to his back, screaming, stunned, eyes rolling in his head. His spearhead fell from his hand and disappeared in a long strand of smoke.

The Llongo jumped into position, surrounding Mala with their shields. Batu bent over him. Mala shook his head, struggled to get up. Batu used an arm to help him.

"It bit me." Mala picked up his right arm with his left hand. "No! Look!" He indicated his palm. "Blisters! It burned me!"

"A fence that burns?" Kantara wondered. "Can such a thing be?"

"You've seen what happens. Leave now."

"Well, now," Tuga smiled, dropping his shield, "here we have a fence we can't go through, and we can't go under. I'll show you how to go over."

He ran at the fence, holding the wooden spear shaft just under the iron head. Tuga had been trained in the Phantom's Jungle Olympics, was pole-vaulting champion of the Llongo, and would have been all-jungle champion if the sensational Wambesi, Banza, had not participated that year. He planted his spear, leaped, soared, twisted gracefully, landed with muscular ease on the other side.

Tuga looked through the fence. His smile was at once self-satisfaction, determination, and menace.

'Throw over my spear," he spoke quietly. "I'll poke out that elusive giant."

"Be careful." Batu arched the spear high in the air. "If he's too dangerous, do not take him alone. Lead him here to our spear points."

"I'll not have trouble." Tuga picked up his spear and turned.

There was a loud crack, a moan from Tuga, and he was dead on his back, a bullet hole over his heart.

This was something the Llongo understood, bullets, rifles. They ran for the protection of rocks and stayed down as bullets raked their hiding places, dusting them with rock chips. After many eternal seconds there was silence.

Then stood Wambara the Shield Bearer, holding high over his head the Peace Shield, bearing the "good" sign of the Phantom. Crossed "P's"? Crossed Sabers?

"We are People of the Peace," Wambara shouted. "We are a peace delegation. We come in peace, not in war. Behold the Phantom's sign."

The chatter of an automatic weapon, and bullets smashed through the shield. Wambara was shocked.

"Are these criminals? Do they not know the sign?"

Batu had one answer. "They do not know our language. Perhaps they are ignorant of everything."

Kantara was not only shocked but indignant. "Why do they shoot at us? We did not hurt their fence. We did not hurt them. Did they kill Tuga for sport?"

Mortars barked a loud cough. Batu had never heard this sound before, but felt it boded nothing good for them.

"Get out!" he yelled. "Back to the canoe."

They fled. And the mortar shells came down into the rocks, blasting, shattering. Fortunately all the shrapnel was contained by the rocks.

As they ran, Kantar shouted, "What about Tuga?"

Batu looked over his shoulder. "He is dead. Nothing worse can happen to him."

Another barrage of mortar shells dropped onto the beach. They buried into the sand, and while they made startling eruptions, they were smothered at the same time.

The Llongo leaped into their canoe, spears clattering on the bottom. The raggedness of their stroke caused the outrigger to zigzag, and the next fall of mortar shells went harmlessly—but terrifyingly—into the water.

CHAPTER 4

The controversy regarding jurisdiction over the Island of Dogs was patently a ridiculous situation, and since the Jungle Patrol had much greater investigative facilities than the Mawitaan Police, it was by mutual consent that Colonel Weeks assumed authority. Indeed his first order of business was to determine just who did have authority over the Island of Dogs. Since such determination was a relatively simple matter for one of his skilled staff, this could very well be a training exercise for a rookie.

Mentally he reviewed the list of new recruits, weighing their assets against the particular job. The name of Riggs came to mind and he seemed eminently suitable. Not only had he obtained a Bachelor of Laws degree, but also a Doctor of Jurisprudence, amply demonstrating his intellectual abilities. On the physical side he had taken a black belt in judo and done quite well in international competition. All in all, an average recruit in the Jungle Patrol. Might work out quite well.

Colonel Weeks depressed an intercom switch, spoke to his aide. "Assignment for the new recruit, Riggs. Determine the ownership and legal status of the Island of Dogs. He is to report directly to me."

Riggs was knocking on the door in the surprisingly short time of forty-five minutes. Colonel Weeks folded his hands and waited for the report, noting that Riggs with his jet-black hair and regular features was a handsome young man. His blue eyes were guileless.

"Sir! The Island of Dogs," Riggs was rigid at attention, "is owned by Major Matthew Helm, resident of this city. Lives at an estate in The Hills country. The island has been owned by a Helm for some three hundred years."

"Thank you. Where did you get the information?"

"Records at Town Hall, sir."

"Intelligent of you to go to the source. Would you have his phone number, too?"

"Yes, sir!" Riggs answered in a loud voice, obviously proud of himself. "I thought he might give me better information than is in the records, so I telephoned there. His granddaughter, Janice Helm, told me he is not available, that his business affairs are in the hands of his lawyer, Lionel Crabbe."

"At ease, Riggs. Call Mr. Crabbe. I'll speak to him. Incidentally, did you find out from the granddaughter where Major Helm is?"

"No, sir," Riggs was crestfallen. "I received the impression he was in Europe."

"Europe is quite large. We of the Jungle Patrol deal in specifics, not generalities. Dismissed, Riggs."

Randolph Weeks hated to belittle the boy, but it wouldn't do to let him get a swelled head. He had to learn his mistakes immediately and gain confidence gradually, after a long series of successes.

"Mr. Crabbe on the phone," the desk intercom interrupted his thoughts. He grabbed the phone and said, "Mr. Crabbe. Colonel Weeks here, Jungle Patrol."

"Yes, Colonel Weeks," was the answer. The tone was clear, precise, yet had a quavering nasal quality that was most irritating. "What can I do for you?"

"I was told you handle Major Helm's business affairs."

"Correct. That's common knowledge."

"Does he own the Island of Dogs?"

"He does."

"It has come to our attention that an electrified fence has been erected around the island. This could be most dangerous. We'd like to discuss it with him."

"Major Helm is not legally responsible for the fence. He leased the island to . . . a seafood company, I believe it was. I have the papers here."

"I see. Would you do me the favor of getting them out of your files? I'd like to look them over. Would this afternoon be all right?"

"I'll be here," Crabbe hung up.

That was rather abrupt, Colonel Weeks thought. Most impolite. In Randolph Weeks experience, people who didn't observe the courtesies in minor things were often slipshod in major things, and this sometimes led either to financial disaster or outright criminality.

Most other men in Colonel Weeks position would have sent over to Crabbe's for the legal papers, but it was axiomatic throughout all ranks of the Jungle Patrol that you never asked another to do what you wouldn't do. Furthermore, Colonel Weeks preferred the personal touch. There were nuances of facial expression, body gestures, intonation and inflections of voice that told more to a skilled interrogator than did words. Of course, the Colonel would be the first to admit that a consummate actor could readily deceive him, as could some types of schizophrenics. However, those who knew him, especially those who knew him to their sorrow, would testify that he couldn't be fooled. Therefore, he whistled up a jeep from the motor pool and drove himself to the lawyer's office.

Lionel Crabbe was long-faced, long-nosed, narrow-eyed, shallow-chinned, had a wisp of a mustache, was balding on the sides of his head while a central strip of hair grew down well towards his forehead. He dressed in the European style of a generation gone: tight-fitting woolen suit, high collar with a clasp, narrow tie, pressed handkerchief in his breast pocket, sharply pointed shoes. He was an anachronism in this area where most wore casual clothes suited to the climate, yet he showed no evidence of discomfort. His manner was also cool; he didn't offer to shake hands, instead gave a curt bow, indicated a chair across from his desk, seated himself and folded his hands.

"How may I help you?"

Colonel Weeks lit his briar and peered through the smoke screen. "I thought we had settled that on the phone."

"Did we?" Crabbe turned his chair slightly so that he stared across the room. "I wasn't aware of it."

Colonel Weeks was patient. "You stated you are Matthew Helm's lawyer. That Matthew Helm owns the Island of Dogs. That the island was leased. That you have the legal documents in your possession."

Lionel Crabbe shifted to stare at another part of the room. "Yes, that is correct."

"I further mentioned that an electrified fence has been erected. This is dangerous and against the public good."

"Were warning signs also erected?"

"So I understand."

"Then," Lionel Crabbe spread his hands and looked at a spot over Colonel Weeks's head, "they are within their rights."

"Do they also have the right to shoot at bathers?"

"If the bathers were uninvited."

"Who are these people?"

"A seafood company. Their express purpose is to develop a new method of packaging their product."

"New methods do not condone the use of guns and electric fences."

Lionel Crabbe turned so he was in profile. At such an angle, his face was remarkably flat. "It's perfectly legal. They derive their rights from Major Helm."

"It may be legal," Colonel Weeks was losing his calm, "but it's still against the public good. Instruct them to remove their gunmen and their fence."

"I couldn't do that . . . not according to the terms of the lease. Perhaps Major Helm could talk to them."

"Where is Major Helm?"

"I don't know. The lease money was paid in advance. He took it and went where he willed."

"What is the name of these people who rented the island?"

"Bering Trans-Ocean Packers."

"Where is their company headquarters?"

"I have no idea. It wasn't necessary for me to learn."

Colonel Week's pipe was puffing like a steam engine. He clenched the bit between his teeth. "I put it to you, Mr. Crabbe, that you are being evasive."

The lawyer's eyes flickered over the Colonel's angry face. He stared away, shrugged his thin shoulders. "You may believe as you will. Everything is legally correct."

"Perhaps. I advise you that if you have pertinent information you are not revealing, it would be to your benefit to reveal it now."

"There is nothing more," Lionel Crabbe said shortly.

Colonel Weeks stood. "We'll be in touch again," he promised. "Keep yourself available."

He drove back to Headquarters thinking that if the interview had not gone as well as he wished, nevertheless he had learned certain things. Lionel Crabbe was withholding information—of that much he was certain. For instance, the check issued to Major Matthew Helm would have had a bank name noted on it, and from that could be deduced the company's main offices. Furthermore, what competent lawyer wouldn't have looked up the credit rating of a firm with whom he was going to do business?

Lionel Crabbe was competent, grant him that. It was his motives that were obscure.

His defensiveness and obliqueness in the matter of the Bering Trans-Ocean Packers would indicate he had a connection with the company. If so, then he had not acted in the best interests of his client—Helm, a punishable offense. There was also a question regarding the ethics of these seafood packers. If they had engaged in illegal acts regarding the lease, then their rental rights were null and void, as their lawyers were undoubtedly aware.

The risk to Bering Packers would seem too big for them to engage in minor collusion with a dishonest lawyer. Surely there were places in the world other than the Island of Dogs suitable for developing their secret process.

Here was a mystery that needed solving. An investigation would have to be made of the island.

Almost as soon as Colonel Weeks returned to his office, the intercom announced that Private Riggs was waiting to see him. The Colonel smiled with satisfaction. Riggs had taken the slight rebuke to heart, but instead of sulking, as many would, he was trying to correct his mistake by working harder. That was the Jungle Patrol way. Every good man had gone through it. So had the Colonel as a rookie. It was part of the training and those who couldn't measure up to the strictest standards left voluntarily. No one had to tell them to go. The proportion of failures, however, was minuscule because of the rigidity of the entrance requirements.

Riggs stamped into the office, saluted smartly, his rigid left arm straight along the seam of his starched shorts.

"Sir. My first report was cursory and did not give you sufficient information to arrive at a decision. Therefore I have spent the intervening time assembling all the available facts."

Colonel Weeks got his briar going, nodded casually. "At ease, Riggs. It will be a welcome change to listen to facts. Give your presentation."

Riggs spread open a map, tacked the corners to the bulletin board. "The Island of Dogs," he pointed to the map's central area, speaking softly, his manner no longer pretentious but informal and instructive. "No water, as you know. As close to a desert island as you'll find. The shoals surrounding it prevent any large ships from even coming near. It's a worthless piece of property and has never been claimed by any modern government. Located out there in the ocean, it's in international waters and has been pretty well ignored by everybody."

"Can we claim jurisdiction in case of a crime?"

"No, sir, not according to international law. Jurisdiction belongs to Major Matthew Helm. He inherited all rights from a direct ancestor who claimed the island for an unknown reason nearly three hundred years ago, and his claim was confirmed by royal grants from five different nations. In actual fact, the present Helm is a dictator, an emperor, has the Divine Right of Kings, and can do anything he wants with the island—except that no one lives there. What gives him all the power is the fact that the island is his personal and private property."

"Hmmm," the Colonel was deep in thought. "It seems he rented it to some seafood packers. Would they have his authority?"

"Yes, sir, they'd be assignees. He can pass on the legal powers he possesses to heirs and assignees."

"Heirs, eh? Well, well. What I'm interested in right now is how's the fishing out there?"

"The Mori haven't complained. They seem to have enough for their own needs and trade. But it's no Grand Banks of Newfoundland. Nothing to attract the trawler fleets."

"Anything that would attract a seafood packer?"

"Nothing discernible, but I don't know much about fishing. These shoals," he circled the island with his pencil, "prevent any landing by ships with over five feet draft. Without larger ships, I don't see how they can do much fishing—or packing. If it's secrecy they're after, it's an ideal place."

"There's a little too much secrecy there. Can we do a flyover?"

"No, sir. It's private property."

Colonel Weeks puffed thoughtfully. "Could Major Helms give us permission?"

"Yes, sir. All leases reserve the right of inspection."

"Then find Major Helm and have him give us authority."

"Unfortunately, sir, the police forces of Europe can't locate him. I wired all of them hours ago with an 'urgent,' and all replies received have been negative."

"Hmm, hmm," smoke puffs rose to the ceiling. "And his lawyer denies knowledge of his whereabouts too. Stranger and stranger. I believe you said there was a niece?"

"A granddaughter. Janice Helm."

"She inherits from him?"

"I haven't seen Matthew Helm's will. It's an assumption."

"A logical assumption. Let's also assume that Matthew Helm is incapable of giving his consent. Janice Helm would have the legal authority to give her consent."

"A tricky point of law. I'd say it's stretching things a bit far."

"Assuring privacy with electric fences and guns is stretching things a bit far. That island is going to be investigated with Janice Helm's consent."

"I'll go visit her, sir," Riggs grinned openly. The hard veneer of the working lawyer dissolved and an eager young man was revealed.

"She must be very lovely," Colonel Weeks commented dryly.

"I wouldn't know, sir. I just spoke to her on the phone."

"Then her voice must be very lovely."

"Like one of the Lorelei, I imagine."

Colonel Weeks threw cold water on Riggs's dream. "She lives in Mawitaan jurisdiction. One of Togando's men will get her written consent."

CHAPTER 5

The jungle trees shivered with the sound of the message. Kettledrums roared like thunder in the mountains, "Phantom come." Tom-toms picked up the phrase and passed it on. "Phantom, Phantom, Llongo call. Llongo dead, Llongo hurt. Phantom come." Mallets beat on hollow logs like so many cannons firing out the words in a continuous relay: "Phantom come. Llongo call. Island of Dogs. Fence that bums. Giant voice. Phantom come."

The booming pounding carried over forests that hadn't been mapped, to the far reaches of the mysterious Misty Mountains, over rivers and lakes and wide savannas where roving beasts reacted by restlessly roaring and pawing. Up and up rose the sound. The winds hurried it. Echoes carried it. Over the Deep Woods, impenetrable to all but the Bandar, the pygmy people of the poison weapons, feared from north to south, east to west. They heard and they listened and they all turned to look at the Skull Cave where sat the Phantom of the Skull Throne, listening to the summons.

Guran, the pygmy leader, turned with a sigh and spoke to the masked man. "The Phantom leaves?"

"Yes. The Jungle Peace has been broken. There is at least one Llongo dead and another hurt. The Law has been violated, Guran."

"The Bandar will be glad to accompany you."

"No, Guran," he answered in his deep voice. "The Island of

Dogs is far from here where people do not understand the ways of the Bandar."

The Phantom rose, settling his holsters on each hip. Time to work. He inhaled, inflating his massive chest, then strode out of the Skull Cave with a light tread peculiar for so large a man; yet when you studied his perfectly proportioned muscularity, you could see how he could carry his giant frame effortlessly.

He mounted Hero, the great white horse of the dancing hooves, whistled for Devil, the iron-jawed, tireless mountain wolf. Down the Phantom Trail they raced. Legends grew from this swift movement. A jungle hunter or a traveler would see a flash of motion and hear a muted sound. In a second it would be gone and on the retina only an insubstantial imprint of a huge man on a great horse followed by a wolf would be left. How the story grew in the telling! And those who had not seen would vie for recognition by inventing a tale surpassing the one of the eyewitness. Then another would tell what he had seen and soon the distinction between truth and fiction blurred.

Now the deep-bellied drums roared a welcome and heralded his approach. "Phantom comes. Prepare, Llongo. Phantom comes."

As the Phantom swung through the palisade gates of the Llongo town, the massed people shouted a welcome that echoed off the faraway Misty Mountains.

The Ghost Who Walks dismounted, went quickly through the crowd to where the exhausted peace delegation sprawled under a thatched shelter. They tried to struggle to their feet, but already the Man Who Cannot Die was among them, waving them down with a soothing yet commanding gesture, his deep voice saying, "Rest, men of Llongo. You did well with the Mori and your journey home was hard. Now I want to hear what happened on the Island of Dogs."

They all started speaking at once.

"Tuga was killed. Shot."

"They shot at us and there were things that exploded in the sand and water."

"I burned my hand."

"The giant's voice kept shouting."

"Hold!" Phantom looked at Batu, the peace-delegation leader. "One at a time. Council talk."

This is the way it was in the Councils of Bangalla. Batu picked up a stick and now no one could talk till the stick was passed to him. Quickly the story came out, and all had a chance to add their personal comments.

Mala undid his bandages, held out his blistered hand. "I

stabbed the fence with my spear, thinking to cut it. See the burns. Here is proof there is a fence of fire, although the fire is invisible."

Phantom nodded. "I know this fire. You are fortunate your spear shaft is of wood."

Wambara indignantly held up the Peace Shield. "See, O Ghost Who Walks. I told them we were People of the Peace. I showed them your Sign. And they shot through it. The scars are here . . . and here . . . and here."

Kantara shook his fist. "We will return to the Island of Dogs with more men. We will recover Tuga's body. We will destroy the giant and the burning fence."

"No, men of Llongo," the Phantom forbade them. "Your spears are no match for automatic rifles and mortar shells. The burning fence and giant voice are mysterious things. The Phantom's Peace was broken. The Law was violated. My Sign was pierced by bullets. It is I who must look into this matter."

He swung onto Hero and spears rose and crashed against shields as he galloped out the gate, Devil at heel. "Phantom! Phantom!" the chorus cheered. All was well in the jungle. The Peace was restored. The crime would be punished by the Ghost Who Walks, as were all serious crimes.

As Hero thundered along the Phantom Trail, the Phantom's thoughts were grim. He knew the barren Island of Dogs and its inimical hostility to life. Why would men go to the trouble and immense expenses of inhabiting it—with all that entailed—then surround it with an electric fence and defend it with modem arms? Why would they do this? Who were these men? What secret did they hide?

While Private Riggs was present, Colonel Weeks was having some serious thoughts too. He studied the written consent signed by Janice Helm on behalf of Matthew Helm and muttered, "We'll have to find out what's happening on that island."

"Sir," Private Riggs interrupted, "you originally consulted me as a lawyer and I'd like to give you a considered opinion. We're on very shaky legal ground here. If Matthew Helm is alive and capable of giving his consent, then the signature of Miss Helm is worthless. He could take us into court for any actions we performed without his specific permission."

"Riggs," Colonel Weeks grinned around his pipe. "Do you think I'd violate the law of the land, or any law for that matter?"

"Well, sir . . . I . . . that is . . . I . . Riggs was a mass of confusion.

The Colonel was amused. "I admit we have a tricky situation

here, as is always the case with private property on which a highly suspicious if not criminal act has occurred. A man's home is his castle—that is the rule throughout the democratic countries of the world. But the beauty of the law is, Riggs, that there is so much of it you can usually find an exception. I believe you said the island is in international waters?"

"Yes, sir!" Riggs sang out for emphasis. "That's what complicates this case. Each nation's interpretation of international law is different, and often shifts according to its own interests. But private property is sacred to all nations. Any action we take, others could see as a threat to their own interests. A matter like this could end up in the World Court at The Hague."

"Riggs, for a young man you have the pessimism of the aged and world-weary."

"I gave you a lawyer's opinion, sir. Of course, as a matter of expediency, we can just walk onto the island, blow a hole in the fence—"

"Riggs!" Colonel Weeks slammed his fist on the desk. "There is no expediency in the Jungle Patrol, only law."

Riggs did more verbal stuttering. "I . . . just . . . sorry. . ."

"I know, I know," the Colonel was somewhat mollified. "You merely parrot the opinion of a large majority of the world. Everybody wants easy solutions to complicated problems. Expediency is the quickest and easiest solution. It doesn't last long, compounds an already confused situation, doesn't even buy time but instead wastes it, yet many people demand an immediate answer and will accept expediency."

Now that they were arguing on an intellectual level about legal technicalities, Riggs lost his embarrassment, even forgot he was a rookie in front of his superior officer. Randolph Weeks admired him for his detachment.

"I might point out there are more laws protecting property than there are protecting people. It isn't surprising that human beings are crying out for equality with dirt."

Colonel Weeks chuckled. "Bravo! Excellent point. Not original, the subject has been broached before by others, in these quarters in fact, and I'll have to give you the answer I gave them. The Jungle Patrol does not make laws. We enforce them. And we obey them."

His face grew stern as he thought back to the time his own daughter had been kidnapped, held in an extraterritorial section of the jungle that had the status of a private nation, and all the Jungle Patrol could do was ring the perimeter and wait. It was degrading that the finest police force in the world was helpless while criminals roistered and boasted almost under their noses. They'd still be standing and waiting, and his daughter would still be a captive, an object of humiliation, if it wasn't for the masked man who left the Skull Mark and was known on the Jungle Patrol's table of organization as the Commander.

He rose, scratching the back of his head with his pipe stem. "We can talk all we want about the actions we could take, but the plain fact is we'll do nothing until we receive orders from the Commander."

"Who, sir?" Riggs exploded in astonishment.

"Our Commander," Weeks replied mildly.

"I thought you were the Commander."

"Officer in Charge, Riggs. That's all."

"Then who's the Commander?"

"It's obvious you're a rookie, Riggs. Veterans never ask that question. It's a waste of breath. No one knows who the Commander is. I don't, and anyone else who says he does is only making a guess."

"But . . . we're taking orders from an ... an unknown."

"Correct. The Patrol was set up that way nearly three hundred years ago, and viewing the system pragmatically, you'll have to admit it works."

"Oh, yes. But how do we receive orders?"

"I'll tell you everything I know," Colonel Weeks opened the office door, "so you won't be bothering your head about it and can get on with your job."

He went out into the corridor, pointed to an office at the end of it. The office was dark. At the bottom corner of the half-glass door, Riggs could barely make out the letters reading: COMMANDER, J.P. RIGGS had believed the office was an adjunct to the Colonel's.

"That's it," Colonel Weeks said. "The Commander's office. As the highest-ranking officer, I have the only key. Only I am permitted in that office. I received the key from my predecessor and will pass it on to my successor. Continuity—that's part of the Patrol. We give orders, Riggs, but the most important part is that we take orders. And obey them."

The Colonel waved his pipe, indicating the light bulb fastened to the wall over the door. "When orders come for us, the light goes on."

Riggs nodded. He had seen the bulb before in the main office of Headquarters, and it was always referred to as the Commander's Light. In the same manner, he had naturally assumed that the control button was in the Colonel's office and when he wanted someone he depressed it. Never for a minute did he think its major function was to summon the Colonel.

He blinked. The light had gone on! Preposterous! A figment of his imagination.

"Amazing!" Colonel Weeks exclaimed. "I've never seen it fail. When we have a puzzling problem, we receive orders from him."

The corridor filled with noise as Major Byrne and Captains de Challon and Van Meergen came running up.

"Sir!" they yelled. "The Commander's Light."

"Yes, yes," Colonel Weeks nodded at them. "We were just talking about it when by coincidence it went on." The pounding of more running feet interrupted him. He used his pipe as a pointer. "Get those men back to their offices, will you? And return to yours, please."

As they left the corridor, he pulled at a chain attached to his belt. The key to the Commander's office slid out of his pocket. Unlocking the door, he said to Riggs, "Wait here. Only I am allowed inside."

And yet, remembering he too was once a rookie, he left the door ajar so Riggs could satisfy his natural and healthy curiosity. Of course there wasn't much in the room that was satisfying. A bare room, one overhead light, no windows, four walls, one safe. That was it.

The Colonel squatted in front of the safe, twiddled the dial. "In case anybody is watching," he spoke aloud, "I alone know the combination to this safe. Our orders from the Commander are received in here."

He swung the door wide, picked up the piece of paper on the bottom that was signed, "Commander," glanced over the message. His face broke into a wide smile.

"Fantastic!" he exclaimed. "Just fantastic! Whenever we have a problem, he anticipates us." He walked out holding the sheet of paper, passed it to Riggs, locked the door again.

Riggs too was amazed at the message. "Give me all information on the Island of Dogs."

"But, sir," he exclaimed. "How did this get in the safe? I mean a bare room, no windows, a locked door at the end of a corridor?"

"I wouldn't worry about it, Riggs. Let's call it a pleasant puzzle. We don't even try to find out. When we joined the Patrol, we all swore an oath of loyalty to the Patrol and its Commander. We stick by that oath. I told you that our obedience to orders is one of our major strengths, and why we have been so effective a force for so long. Why don't you get on that report, Riggs?"

"Me, sir?"

"Of course. You did all the investigative work. Very fair job.

And sign the report with your name and rank, will you Riggs?"

"Yes, sir!" Private Riggs replied.

The Phantom was in a deserted section on the outskirts of Mawitaan, a section deserted because of fear. Not even thieves and thugs took refuge from the law here. The enemy of life was here. Death was here.

All the wells of the area were contaminated. A simple thing like washing one's hands was tantamount to suicide. How the wells had become poisoned was lost in history; it must have been gradual because the emptying of the quarter was gradual.

Not all of the wells were poisoned; at least one wasn't because it wasn't a well at all, but rather a false well, an underground entrance to an old tunnel that connected this area to Jungle Patrol Headquarters. The rocks lining this abandoned well were cleverly placed so that footholds were there for those who knew—and only the line of Phantoms knew. The passage itself was rock-hewn, and exited under the Commander's room in Jungle Patrol Headquarters. In fact, it exited under the safe. Bolts held the heavy steel bottom that swung down in order that messages could be delivered and obtained.

The solid rock passage had been cut by long dead ancestors. Only the Chronicles of the Phantom recorded their secret labors. Indeed, the very fact the Jungle Patrol had been founded by the Phantom was known only in the Chronicles. And every Phantom since the Sixth roared with laughter when he read that the First Officer in Charge was none other than Redbeard.

Redbeard, the notorious pirate whose world-shaking deeds rang through history. Redbeard, who would sail under no flag—all his bloodthirsty fleet needed as a fighting ensign was his beard flying in the wind as he stood in the prow of his vessel. Redbeard, Scourge of the Sea, Flail of the Land. A strange combination of cruelty and kindness, of honor and deceit, of sinner and saint.

He was a man, a great and powerful leader whom men gladly followed. Yet in an epic fight, the sixth of the line of Phantoms defeated him. Folklore had the names mixed up and even the events. The tales were used to scare children. Redbeard had become an evil force out to devour the world and only a lone man stood between him and annihilation. Mountains crashed down, valleys were formed as they dug in their heels and were pulled yea and nea, seas were emptied and continents up-heaved in their struggle. Their laborious inhalations caused deserts and their exhausted exhalations put clouds around the world. See, they're still there, my child. Evil ripped up Earth, threw it at Man, and we have the moon. The Great Rift was caused when Man threw Evil on his back. In the titanic struggle that lasted for centuries, Man defeated Evil, and Peace came to the world.

The truth was noted prosaically by the Sixth in the Chronicles. The sixth Phantom challenged the undefeated Redbeard to a sword duel and defeated him. So it was written. The Sixth gave him another chance in hand-to-hand combat and defeated him. So it was written.

But what could be read between the few simple lines of writing! Redbeard, historically acknowledged the finest swordsman of his day, who himself made the law that only an undefeated man could rule the pirate fleets and further stated that any man could challenge him, who fought to the death on a daily basis, whose speed and power kept him alive for years and years, kept him in his position as admiral of the pirate ocean and king of sword-won domains. Yet the Sixth knocked the sword out of his giant's grasp.

It was a matter of historical record that the young Redbeard in a critical moment lifted the mast of a fighting ship and stepped it into place. By inference he was acknowledged the strongest man in the world. He didn't need rope and pulleys to warp a ship's cannon into place; he lifted the carriage and skidded it along the deck—there were eyewitnesses to this. Yet Redbeard became a sleeping baby when the Sixth's steel fist crashed into his jaw.

There was an ancestor to be proud of. And thereafter Redbeard devotedly served the only man who defeated him, became the First Officer in Charge of the Jungle Patrol. He tried to undo the wrongs he had done. With his pirates at his back—and now members of the Patrol—he swarmed into pirate lairs and rooted them out of the Bangalla coast. Always Redbeard was at the Sixth's command, right up until the day he died, grinning as his blood drained from dozens of wounds and he fell forward, his jacket releasing the head of his implacable enemy, Akmehd, rightly called the Curse of God.

Never again was there an officer in charge such as Redbeard, but after he was done never was such another needed. He didn't eliminate all crime, but he and the Sixth did much to smash piracy on the Bangalla coast by denying the pirates their land bases. Only later generations had time to record events in the Jungle Patrol Log; therefore, the origins of the Jungle Patrol were hazy and Colonel Randolph Weeks never suspected he was a military descendant of the wild, free looter, Redbeard.

Private Riggs typed his report carefully, using legal terseness and stating only the facts he had obtained. On presenting it to

Colonel Weeks, the Colonel read it through, nodding his approval. "Good work. Everything's here."

They went out into the corridor. The light over the Commander's office was still on and would stay on till the Commander received the desired report. Once more Colonel Weeks went through the unlocking routine, and except for placing the report in the safe, everything was much the same as when they had received the Commander's message.

"But," Riggs asked, "how will we know he gets the report?"

"The light," the Colonel indicated it. "It goes off."

"It seems a very awkward way of delivery."

"It's the way he chooses."

"But how can we reach him in an emergency?"

"Carrier pigeon," was the laconic answer.

"Carrier pigeon?" Riggs thought he was being joshed but a glance at the Colonel's bored expression told him he had made this same explanation many times. "Carrier pigeon," he repeated. "Surely there's a better way."

"Perhaps there is. Radio's not certain during electrical storms, and we have more than our share of them. From experience we know the pigeons reach him."

"Where is he?"

Colonel Weeks waved vaguely with his pipe towards the jungle. "Somewhere there. The birds fly in that direction. It's not important."

Riggs felt very dissatisfied with the answers.

The Phantom retrieved the report from the safe, walked back through the tunnel to daylight. Sitting on the floor of a roofless house, Hero on one side, Devil on the other, he read through it. When he came to the "fact" of Matthew Helm's irrefutable claim to the Island of Dogs, his quick mind saw the flaw in the "irrefutability," and he roared with laughter. Hero pranced and Devil danced at his burst of humor.

"He received royal grants from five sovereigns. Ridiculous! It means none of them wanted it, and it wasn't theirs to give. If Matthew Helm wants to base his claim on prior rights, I can prove the First set foot on the island a hundred years before a Helm saw it. Down, Hero! Sit, Devil! Control yourselves. I have to finish reading this."

A few minutes later he nodded his head. It was a good report. This Private Riggs thought clearly, except when it came to understanding the spuriousness of Helm's claim. Still, even that was understandable. Most people were dazzled by such things as royal grants. They didn't understand that the most powerful monarch who ever lived couldn't give away what wasn't his. Yet many a famous king was profligate with his royal grants—they were much cheaper than cash, and if it involved property that didn't belong to them, so much the cheaper.

The Phantom wrote on a small pad of the Commander's official stationery. His orders, like General Grant's, were a model of brevity and clarity.

"Send Private Riggs by helicopter over Island of Dogs. Purpose: observation only; no landing. Report sightings to me."

Private Riggs was in the lounge of the modern barracks, stunned by the succession of secrets revealed to him: the unknown Commander; the locked room; the Commander's Light; the safe. His expression must have showed his bewilderment. The other Patrolmen had gone through the experience, and now they joked with him in many languages—a Patrolman who didn't speak at least three languages besides his native tongue was considered rather dull.

"*Mes frères*," Villon asked his comrades, "is there not a certain look of stupidity in this poor one's eyes?"

Torson laughed his huge laugh. "I thought t'at was t'e way he was issued to us—stupid-looking."

"Ere now, cobber," Kelly the Australian put a protective arm around Riggs, "if you want to look stupid, you just go right ahead."

"I say now," Hattieford protested, "you chaps are going a bit far. He can't be stupid. He passed his tests. It must be his usual expression."

"*Dio mio!*" Cellini threw up his arms. "You mean I have to gaze upon that for the extension of my enlistment?"

Stavros stood by Rigg's side, held up a restraining hand. "Please!" he implored. "Please! Under Athenian Democracy every man has a right to speak in his own defense."

"Like Socrates?"

"He spoke too much."

"Nothing like the good old American way," Carson drawled. "Give 'em a fair trial and hang 'em."

"I say, let's 'ang 'im and then give 'im a fair trial."

"Gentlemen, please! You insult Stavros with these remarks of little consequence. We must hear from the young one. Speak, *kyrios*."

"I . . . er . . . ." Riggs stammered.

"You see," Stavros glanced around proudly, "he does speak. "Not melodic Greek perhaps, only the tongue of you *barbaroi*—"

"Boo!" Kelly started it. A shower of pillows and wadded paper rained on Stavros. He fled, head between arms, then leaped on a table, wrapped an imaginary cloak around himself, threw back his head proudly, pointed a finger skywards in an exaggerated rhetorical gesture.

"Heap me with your debris," he rolled out the words in mock-declamatory style. "Bury me under stones, you peasants. Nothing can quell the inner spirit that burns within me."

"I can speak Ancient Greek," Riggs came to the defense of Stavros, speaking mildly to the nearest person. It happened to be Hattieford, the Englishman. He turned, smiled slightly.

"Don't ruin Stavros's finest hour, there's a good chap."

"But he—"

"He's perfectly capable of taking care of himself. He happens to have a doctorate in psychology. Don't you see what he's done? He diverted their minds from you to himself. Clever chap, what? Might want to take notes."

The crowd tired of fencing with Stavros; he was much too nimble-witted, he had a certain boomerang quality that turned your own humor back on you. They trickled back to the tables to study, play chess, read, otherwise mentally amuse themselves in their free time. Torson clapped Riggs on the shoulder with a huge paw.

"Hey, youngster, I hear you play yudo. We go to yim some night, have few falls, yah?"

Riggs looked him over, measuring him. Torson was immense. Those types didn't have the proper balance; he'd fall like a foundationless wall. Riggs nodded slowly, already seeing the leg sweep and quick tug he'd use to put Torson on his back in a little under a second. Everyone there saw the calculating look in his eye, and all promised silently they'd be in the gym when these two met.

Torson also saw the change in Riggs's manner. He peered closer, the vacancy of the oaf gone from his eyes and quick intelligence replacing it. He laughed his booming laugh.

"Ho! I t'ink I bite off too much. You excuse Old Tor, t'e Hammerthrower, yah? Sometime," he tapped his great round skull, "I act too stupid."

Riggs remembered back to the last Olympics, to the fabulous Swede the newspapers quickly dubbed Tor the Hammer, whose every practice throw broke a world record. As in all sports, agility counted quite as much as muscle and Tor would be a formidable adversary in the judo circle. He wouldn't be off balance at all. Fortunately, here he was offering his friendship and Riggs suddenly realized he'd just passed a test much stiffer than any he had taken to enter the Jungle Patrol. He had been tried and found satisfactory. He had stood the joshing, but more important was that as a judo champion of international reputation he hadn't insisted on competing against Torson to enhance his own reputation and belittle the giant. He demonstrated he was a man. Now he was accepted in the camaraderie of the Jungle Patrol.

Villon sprawled in a chair, as lazy as a well-fed lion who wouldn't tolerate anything more than flies. "*Mon ami*," he smiled tight-lipped. "I would not bother the brain over the precise identity of the Commander. You stay around long ee-nough, you deescovair that thees Commandair know three, four, five time more than you do. The sparrow, it does not fly with the hawk. Be content you are in the company of those who can fly, eh?"

Captain Van Meergen stuck his head in the door. "Riggs? Report to Colonel Weeks on the double."

"Oh, oh," Torson frowned. "I do not think the Colonel summons you to whisper more secrets. Be careful, youngster."

CHAPTER 6

Janice Helm sat by the swimming pool, tanning her already bronzed body. She was magnificent in every way with a blond, blue-eyed beauty. She was also bored, and in Janice Helm that could be very dangerous. There was in her the streak of recklessness that ran through all the Helm family, and she added to it a disregard of convention that made her unique in European student circles. For instance, as far as was known she was the only girl who had ever climbed the spires of King's College Chapel at Cambridge and from its top flown her liberated bra. For this she was dismissed from Gorton College, she being deemed the only one physically and mentally capable of such an act

Her being "sent down" as her fellow students called the expulsion, led to marches of protest. It might have led to more serious deeds if she hadn't huffily declared that this antiquated arena (with some of the most modern laboratories in the world) wasn't sufficient to contain all her talents.

Janice Helm was precociously brilliant—as they found out to their sorrow at the University of London. She could absorb tremendous masses of information if it were necessary to further her schemes—or pass an important test— otherwise she didn't bother to study. Her theories on economics were more reckless than her spending sprees, but often her observations were amazingly astute. As to the classics, she neatly divided the classical world into two and set them arguing.

She "discovered" an Icelandic saga, written in ancient Runic on antique vellum, concerning the deeds of that doughty warrior Ossian riding through Ireland. All critics agreed the poetry and imagery were exquisite, but certain mistakes in spelling had been made that some classicists refused to attribute to a centuries-dead scribe. So the classic world separated and hurled themselves at each other. Janice Helm, the authoress, enjoyed herself immensely by writing opinions, under various names, that favored each side.

Casually, in the Ashmolean Library, she placed a "lost" page of the Domesday Book which "proved" that William the Conqueror had parceled out land where London now stood to families still surviving. The courts were in a turmoil before that was straightened out.

While the legal battles were still raging, Janice decided to start another controversy by writing a letter to the London *Times* stating that Great Britain should discard Parliament and return to Absolute Monarchy. At the same time, she posted another letter (again using a pseudonym) to the *Manchester Guardian* advocating that the Throne and Parliament should be abolished and government run by workers' councils.

Now there was an argument politicians could get their teeth into. As a matter of fact, every politician thought it was the perfect argument on which to debate: the battlelines were neatly drawn and ninety-nine percent of the voters were in the middle. They could come out squarely for motherhood and take a firm stand against sin. Duplicators and mimeographs clacked day and night issuing dozens of "positive stands." The postal authorities were swamped. The BBC commented on the fervid turmoil. Politicians demanded time to state their views. The *Times* and the *Guardian* stated they would report on the situation but they would no longer print commentaries. Local radio stations felt like they were under siege.

Eventually, when authorship of all the public and semiprivate disturbances were traced back to Janice Helm, she grinned at them and said, "Well, you weren't bored, were you?"

Half the country howled with laughter, and the other half howled for her head. Another controversy was in the making, and this time she wasn't responsible. Not directly, anyway.

It was decided for her that the educational climate at the Sorbonne would be much more compatible with her temperament, and there were rumors a scholarship fund was provided for her—although, truth to tell, these rumors could just as well have been false as true—and there was the fact Janice Helm was fiercely independent and never accepted anything for nothing.

Ah, Paris. Paris in the spring. Paris in the fall. Paris any time at all. Janice was quickly assimilated into the international society of the Sorbonne students. They saw nothing odd about her at all, to them she was just one of the ordinary people, a bit outspoken perhaps, but certainly not radical.

Janice was indignant. She had to prove she was an individual. What she did to accomplish this became known to the newspapers of France as *l'Affaire de la Femme Fatale*.

Janice's first move was to start a student newspaper. It should be noted here that all her escapades involved literature in one form or another, and that she had a genuine literary talent. There was no way she was going to let her newspaper be lost in the morass of sameness, be just another college newspaper with a lot of complaints, nothing constructive, news that everyone knew two weeks ago.

Eminently suitable for Janice's plan was that the French Minister of Information had a seventeen-year-old son who was at that very awkward stage of being a boy trapped in a man's body. René was intelligent but he was sadly lacking in experience outside the classroom or off the soccer field. Of course he firmly believed he was worldly-wise, having picked up so much wisdom from his boasting peers who were themselves victims of misinformation. He was more of a victim than an unwitting accomplice.

What could such a handsome young man do when a gorgeous blonde in an alluring black dress swept in his direction, held out a cigarette in a half-meter-long holder, and breathed in a husky contralto, "Light?"

René almost set the Comédie Français on fire before he had Janice's cigarette lit. After clearing his throat a number of times of a particularly obstinate obstruction, he squeaked, "Would you like to join me in my box?"

Since his voice had vacillated a full octave in one sentence, he tried it again, holding it to a steady baritone. "Only the President's is superior as to view."

"No," Janice let drift a cloud of smoke, and peered archly through it, "Moliére bores me."

"Moliére!" René shouted at the insult to the Shakespeare of France. Then he remembered he was portraying the part of the suave man bored with the world. "Yes," he drawled. "So gauche, don't you think?"

That started it. A week later, Janice was telling him, "René, you are absolutely ignorant of the real world. You are living in a dream. Throw away your child's books and take a look at reality."

René promptly went home, took a look at his father's private papers, and next day knowledgeably discussed them with Janice. In turn, she wrote a column in her paper, called "From the Crystal Ball," and her predictions proved to be so outstandingly accurate that she was offered jobs on newspapers in Paris, and a number of enterprising reporters cultivated her friendship—much to the detriment of their pride and expense accounts.

The information she printed had little value except that it had not been released yet. Janice's intention was to point out governmental absurdity regarding needless secrecy, and in this she succeeded admirably. It really was of little consequence who had been transferred to what department, yet bureaucrats stamped "Secret" on transfers, and said that premature revelations were a danger to the state. Of course, the individual concerned knew, as did those associated with him, naturally his superiors were very much cognizant, wives gossiped as they shopped in the rue Faubourg St. Honoré, it was common knowledge in the histros where farewell parties were held, there was even one case where farewell speeches were prematurely delivered in public and were televised—still, having to read it first in a student newspaper, that was too much.

René was severely chastised, his father was told to keep his papers in his safe (what safe? he protested; they had never given him one) and Janice was given her passport, escorted to the Italian border, and she enrolled at the University for Foreigners at Perugia.

For a while all went well, but Janice grew bored again. This time there was the discovery of a lost Ariosto manuscript indicating that he was really William Shakespeare. It caused a little ripple of interest, then the question was asked if Janice Helm was in the vicinity. When the answer was affirmative, all became calm in the classical world. A pity, too, because Janice Helm stoutly maintained she had nothing to do with the Ariosto manuscript. Perhaps he really was William Shakespeare? Everybody else took credit for his works, why not Ariosto?

What she certainly was responsible for came to be known in the university as the Malodorous Affair. A certain mathematics professor would write an equation on the blackboard, start drawing a conclusion from it, encourage students to give him the succeeding equations, then just before the final equation which would give him the logical conclusion came forth, he'd turn around, put his right forefinger alongside his nose, hold out his left hand waist-high, and shout, "Aha! I smell something."

One day he did indeed. He turned around, left hand extended, and Janice Helm put a laboratory bottle on it, removing the cork.

The smell! You gagged. It gripped you by the throat and choked you. It clung. It dripped. It smothered. To inhale seemed to risk death; you didn't want it near your lungs. No alchemist had ever brewed such a vile concoction. It repelled. In fact, it had certain propellant powers—everybody within range of it ran.

And here was this nameless professor with a handful of it, not knowing what to do with it. The cork was gone with Janice Helm and the rest of the class.

You might say he should have corked the bottle with a twist of paper. Or put it on the desk and laid a light book across its mouth. But you weren't there enduring the nasal agony. Or were you? Perhaps the professor should have done these things, but all hindsight is 20-20 vision. The French have a term for it: the wit of the staircase. As you leave an office or a girl, you go down the stairs and mutter to yourself, I should have said this, I should have said that, and you can think of all manner of brilliant repartee— when you're on the staircase, too late to display how wittily intellectual you really are.

The professor did what you and I would have done when assaulted with this odoriferous chemical weapon. He ran to the window and threw the bottle out Unfortunately, passing below was an old open truck heading for the genetics laboratory with 988 field mice loaded on the back, each in a handmade cage. The bottle, as it was tossed, turned over and over, copiously spraying the truck.

The driver fled. The truck crashed into a stone pillar. The fragile cages broke. The field mice, all of them tainted with the witches' brew, fled into the campus and down the nearest holes....

At the University of Copenhagen, Janice dated a young history professor who guided her through the scholastic maze and encouraged her to take additional courses. Their dates turned more into research projects than what could be ordinarily called a date. Therefore, at the age of twenty, Janice graduated—with honors. She grabbed her diploma and flounced away irritably. Given another few months, her history professor had been about to discover that Holger Danske—the Danish folk hero—had really been a Swede.

Now Janice was bored again. Sitting by her grandfather's swimming pool while he toured Europe was not her idea of fun. Furthermore, she had a problem. Somewhere, somewhere in this wide world, there must be a man she could marry.

Admittedly her standards were high. He had to be tall,

handsome, strong, intelligent, capable, wealthy, and dominant in a quiet way. A lack of any of these assets would render him ineligible. If only her grandfather were home, she'd go out searching for this one man rather than sit around waiting. Good grief! How long could a girl wait? Why, she was practically an antique. The dream boy might not want her by the time she showed up.

Gooley, the Llongo maid, came out on the patio. She, too, was a very attractive girl and she was more companion to Janice than maid. They had been children together and it annoyed Janice that they had to grow up in two such different worlds, whereas Gooley thought her own world was the best world and felt sorry that Janice had to endure the many complications of a life-style that should have been basically simple.

"Time to dress, miss," she smiled her very intriguing smile. "Cook serving soon."

"Why dress?" Janice shrugged her bikini top. "No one's here."

"Major Helm is very strict about that."

"Gooley, Granddad is not only from a different generation, he's from a different century. Tell Cook to forget the big formal meal. Make cold cuts or something. We'll all eat out here."

Gooley's frown of disapproval was interrupted by the doorbell ringing. In a minute she returned, followed by two very large men who either wore clothes that were too small or were too big for their clothes. The latter was most probably correct. The arms of their suit jackets bulged where their muscles strained the material. The suits had a lumpy appearance because of the muscularity of their wearers, both of whom were so broad across the chest they had to leave their coats unbuttoned.

One had a moustache and seemed somewhat fleshier than the other, who looked like he had been carved from the side of a granite cliff, and who, when the last cut was made, freeing him, just walked away. The fact that the one with the moustache was brunette and the granite man was blond was incidental to the rest of their striking appearances.

Janice wasn't afraid of these formidable men, she was more annoyed that Gooley hadn't announced them so she could have put a robe on and greeted them inside. Then she noticed both of them held Gooley by an elbow. Janice sat up straight, pulling a towel across her shoulders.

The Moustache lumbered forward, holding out an envelope in a huge hand that looked like the bones had been broken in a number of places and healed badly.

"Got a message from Mr. Helm," he said in a heavy

guttural accent.

Janice nodded, took the envelope, removed the message, glanced at it quickly. It was simply worded.

> Dear Janis
> Come with these men.
> I am ill.
> Major Helm

Janice's first reaction was one of panic. Her grandfather was sick. She had to go to him at once. Then she noticed the greeting again. Janis! Would her own grandfather have misspelled her first name? Of course not. And he certainly wouldn't have signed himself "Major Helm." It was always "Granddad," and he always sent his "Love."

The letter was a forgery. She had to get away. Except the huge, hulking Granite Man was standing right in the path of her flight.

He must have sensed her suspicion. He reached down for her, clutching.

The helicopter hummed loudly through the air, staying close to the water. The pilot nodded at a rock on the horizon. "There it is. The Dogs. Want me to skim in close?"

"No. Strict orders from the Colonel. Observe only and be careful. Circle the island and then we'll fly a search pattern."

The pilot nodded, gained altitude, started his first circle. Riggs put his binoculars to his eyes. There was the electric fence as reported. Height of rocks on one side, a bowl depression beyond the fence and—WOW!

"Hey!" Riggs yelled. "Look at that." He swept his magnified sight up and down the island.

Concrete blockhouses. High towers. Barracks. Warehouses. Cranes. Oil storage tanks. Concrete roads. A factory. Two factories. An oceangoing ship sidled up to a pier.

"That's an experimental laboratory?" Riggs wondered aloud. "They look like they're in production already. Heavy production. Just look at all those barracks. There must be a thousand men living down there."

The pilot could see it all with the naked eye, and nodded agreement. He stopped the circle he was making and bored in, dropping low for a closer look.

A black smoke-blossom grew in front of them, and the helicopter swayed wildly as the concussion of a blast hit it.

Sergeant MacGregor, the pilot, hauled it around, struggling for control.

"Flak!" he yelled.

"Flak!" Riggs echoed. "Why? They can't do that, can they?"

In answer, two more bursts of flak appeared in the air, one to the fore and one to the aft. MacGregor brought the aircraft all the way around, put it into a dive to gain speed, and headed for home with the safety valve buttoned down. Three more flak puffs exploded in places they had vacated seconds before, chasing them and bouncing them.

"They can do it," MacGregor shouted, "and they are." He brought the chopper close to the water, down below the level of the electric fence, in what he considered to be a safe zone.

Riggs was too indignant to be scared. He spun around in his seat glaring at the receding Island of Dogs. "How dare they shoot at an unarmed plane on a peaceful mission? I've a good mind to go back—"

"You'll go alone, laddie." MacGregor eyed his dials. "Those weren't amateur gunners shooting at us, they were professionals. They could have shot the buttons off us if they'd a mind to. The first series of bursts plainly said, 'No Trespassing.' The second series read, 'Get Out of Here,' and I had a mind to obey them."

"Well," Riggs was still angry, "I'm going to tell the Colonel about this."

"Aye," MacGregor commented dryly. "You do that."

Colonel Weeks listened to Private Riggs's report with stony-faced silence. At the conclusion, he commented, "An anti-aircraft gun on the Island of Dogs?"

"At least two, sir. Sergeant MacGregor says the gunners knew their business, could have knocked us out of the sky without any trouble, but were just giving us a warning."

"Odd that a seafood plant should feel the need of antiaircraft guns."

"Sir, I don't know anything about seafood packing, but that doesn't look like a fish factory."

"Concrete barracks, you said. An indication of permanency, not a temporary base."

"And an oceangoing vessel at a pier that seemed permanent to me. They must have blasted a passage through the reefs."

Colonel Weeks had his pipe going full steam as he led the way from the landing pad to Headquarters. "Riggs," he declared angrily, "I believe your original idea was correct— blow a hole through the fence, wade in there, see what's going on. Can't do it, of course. The most difficult thing in life is to be patient."

"What can we do, sir?" Riggs followed the Colonel into the office.

"Nothing." Colonel Weeks took the swivel chair behind his desk. "Wait till the Commander reads the report, gives us further orders."

The phone rang. Colonel Weeks was annoyed, snatched at it. "Yes!" he said more gruffly than he intended.

A deep voice he recognized at once was on the other end. "Colonel Weeks? This is the Commander. I wish to speak to Private Riggs."

The Colonel bolted out of his chair, stood at attention, "Yes, sir. He's standing right here, sir."

"No, I wish to interview him personally. He is to drive out of Mawitaan to the Twin Forks. He is to take the right fork, drive along it for precisely four and seven-tenths miles by the odometer."

"But, sir, that leads to the Jungle of Night."

"Correct. Set your watch. I will see Riggs exactly two hours from now." A click on the phone indicated the conversation had ended.

Colonel Weeks cradled the phone thoughtfully. Riggs interrupted his train of ideas. "Sir, was that the Commander?"

"What?" Weeks blinked. "Who? . . . oh . . . yes, yes, it was the Commander. Always a shock to hear him. You will. He wants to see you."

"See me?"

"Yes. Orders. Get ready. I'll give you your directions later."

Riggs gulped audibly. He was going to see the Commander. He wondered if anyone in the Jungle Patrol had ever stood face-to-face with the Commander. Probably not. Otherwise they certainly would have talked about it.

By the time he finished his hurried preparations, he shined. His shoes were mirrors. The uniform was freshly cleaned and pressed, its creases like knifeblades. Even the leather chin strap that went across the front brim of his pith helmet reflected light

He picked up a jeep at the motor pool, drove to Twin Forks, took the right hand turn and checked his odometer. He wondered why the Colonel had referred to this area as the Jungle of Night. Seemed perfectly normal. The blacktop road wasn't bad, needed a few repairs, but the little he had heard about this part of the country was that it was sparsely populated.

The road petered out to a trail at the same time it became twilight. Confused, he checked his watch. There was no logical reason for the gathering darkness . . . till he glanced overhead.

The thickly growing trees were forming an arch of branches, and the branches supported vines, and the vines supported creepers, and the creepers supported suckers, and the suckers supported shootlings. Through this dense mat, the sun could barely shine; it was much like stars on a bright night. And ahead was a tunnel of blackness.

Riggs put on the headlights, and drove slowly. Now he knew why this section was referred to as the Jungle of Night. He had seen few nights darker. Intellectually, he realized that the sun was blazing overhead, nourishing all the growth at ground level, yet as he rode through damp blackness he couldn't convince his body, his eyes, that it wasn't night. All his senses said it was. He clung to his slender thread of rational knowledge to keep himself from turning and roaring out of there at full speed, back to the day, back to the sun.

The lighted odometer showed exactly four and seven-tenths miles. He stopped, shut off the engine. Immediately the noises of the jungle pressed in on him.

This was a killer's world. All the nocturnal predators prowled through it. He heard the low hunger-moan of the hunting leopard as it tiptoed along tree branches. Distinctly he heard the cough of a tiger. The great constrictors slithered through the trees. Howler monkeys shriekingly proclaimed their insanity in the high world, picking fruit while the meat-eaters strained to reach them. Below the earth, thousands of species of insects churned and thrummed and screeched squeakily and clattered nightmare fangs. The noise was deafening and occasionally it was punctuated by the scream of a dying animal.

Suddenly all sound stopped as though a switch had been thrown. The silence was eerie, even more threatening, as though everything in the jungle were suddenly afraid of something more deadly than they themselves. Riggs's hand was stealing towards the rifle in the compartment on the side of the jeep.

From the darkness came a voice, a deep resonant voice, "Private Riggs!" It was a statement, not a question.

"Y—yes . . . sir," Riggs had throat problems again. He tried to peer into the darkness. It was impossible. He didn't even know where to look. There was a quality to the voice, a reverberation perhaps, that made it omni-directional.

"What did you see when you flew over the Island of Dogs?"

"Hundreds of men working. Bulldozers. Excavations. Cement trucks. Rail lines and rail cars." Riggs went on and on with the inventory. He was sure he covered everything.

Then he found out how little he told and how much he

knew. The questions came flying at him.

The freighter—what was her estimated tonnage? Was she flying a flag? Any identification? What was her power, steam or diesel? The anti-aircraft, guns—what caliber? Automatic, semiautomatic, manually loaded? Radar-controlled, sight-controlled? Type of fuses, radio or time? Type of shells, high-explosive, phosphorous, smoke? The electric fence—did it surround the island or was it just on the beach side? The passageway blown through the reef—could he tell how deep and how far out it extended by the color change of the water?

This deep voice went on at the same tone and pace, patiently waiting for answers. You could feel the spear-point mind behind it, shucking all unnecessary verbiage, camouflage, deception, going straight to the heart of each subject.

It asked, "Do you know the various types of cranes?"

"I think so."

"Think carefully, Riggs. There were cranes there. What kinds?"

Riggs was reliving those few instants he had had with the binoculars. "Near the dock," he monotoned, "unloading the ship was a hammerhead crane."

"Was there a gantry?"

"I can't be sure. Looked like transporter cranes on the railroad tracks. Two . . . three of them. Then there were some towers that might have been traveling towers, again I can't be sure."

"Any cherry-pickers?"

Riggs gasped. The implication of this was something you didn't want to think about. "No, sir!" he exploded.

"Your report," the deep voice continued evenly, "stated the Island of Dogs came under no official control." The quick change of subject was a psychological trick, and Riggs was too confused to recognize it as a method of diverting his mind from an unpleasant subject.

"Yes, sir," Riggs replied with certainty. "Not even the Jungle Patrol has legal status there."

"That's all, Riggs," the quiet voice stated. "Return to Headquarters." The directive had all the authority of a booming command.

Riggs sat there for a moment, trying to gather his wits, when just as suddenly as the jungle had quieted it burst into sound again. The chitterings and coughings and screechings and screamings were all around him. He suddenly realized he was alone, that the Commander had left as noiselessly as he had come. The first thought Riggs had was, What kind of man was the

Commander that even the jungle predators feared him and were quiet when he passed?

Turning the jeep around, he went as fast as possible, and sighed with relief when he reached the zone of twilight. He hadn't realized he was sweating.

At Headquarters, Colonel Weeks summoned him. It was not another interrogation, nor idle curiosity; it was a search for knowledge.

The Colonel sat back in his chair, puffed on his pipe. "You saw the Commander, Riggs?"

"No, sir. Just heard him. It was dark."

"Should have warned you about that. Thought you would have learned it during your indoctrination course."

"I did, but only in the abstract. The reality was something different."

"Entirely different," Colonel Weeks permitted himself a wry smile, remembering some of his own experiences in the Jungle of Night. "Well then, did he give any orders to the Patrol, any orders at all?"

"No, sir, none. He didn't say he was going to handle the matter himself, I just got that impression."

"Hmmm, yes. How did he sound?"

Marshaling his impressions and ideas, Riggs didn't answer for a minute. How to describe the Phantom's voice? It was like trying to describe the sea to desert dwellers. They couldn't comprehend that there was an abundance—even an overabundance—of a scarce and precious commodity. Riggs chose his words carefully.

"Well, sir, I'd guess a great general would have sounded like that. Or a great king. Someone supremely confident in his own abilities. They don't have to give a direct command. You want to obey. It's a privilege to serve."

Colonel Weeks nodded with understanding.

"Yes, he sounds that way to me. Even on the radio and telephone."

CHAPTER 7

The Phantom was coming to some conclusions of his own, based upon the written and verbal reports given by Private Riggs. His mind closed on facts and went straight to conclusions.

Why would a seafood company, even one with a secret process to protect, resort to electric fences, automatic rifles, mortars, and anti-aircraft guns? It was absurd.

And this secret process—did it demand heavy equipment of the kind described by Riggs? Rail tracks, concrete barracks, transporter cranes, ultimately blowing a passage through shoal waters to bring in ocean freighters. Surely a company engaged in experimental processes would keep expenses to a minimum, erect temporary living quarters and perform most transportation by trucks and not by rail line. The physical description given of the Island of Dogs by Riggs spoke of permanency, whereas the development of a secret process was by its very nature a project that was limited in scope and time. Therefore, a myth was being created and a lie perpetrated. But why? That was the basic question.

The man who knew most about it was Major Helm. He was reported to be vacationing in Europe. However, his granddaughter was at his estate in The Hills section of Mawitaan, and it was possible she could supply a good deal of missing information.

Janice Helm was having her own problems at the moment. The Granite Man was reaching for her, massive hands open to grab her. She was used to eluding grasping clutches, and slid off the webbed chaise lounge with the suppleness of an eel, wriggled under his arms, pivoted out to clear space. At the same time she yelled a warning, "Gooley!"

Gooley could neither help nor run. The Moustache had a firm grip on her, and pushed her in a chair, ripping off her apron to use as an impromptu rope. Gooley's struggle was a waste of energy.

Janice was putting her energy to excellent use. The Granite Man made an attempt from behind to wrap a thick arm around her. She used the high heel of her slipper to kick him under the knee, rammed her elbow backwards and stabbed him in the stomach. He started hopping around, doubled over, arms wrapped around his middle. Janice ran towards the house.

Immediately the Moustache leaped in front of her like a bounding ape. With a degree of speed more than equal to his, she bunched her small right fist and planted it squarely on his jaw. It stopped him for but a fractional second—his thick neck absorbed most of the punch—yet the important thing was that he was stopped and Janice was flying past him.

"Get her!" the Granite Man roared.

"I'm trying," the Moustache yelled back.

The Granite Man took a couple of huge leaping running steps and caught Janice by the elbows. Promptly she thrust her high heel down on his instep. He howled in agony. "She's crippling me."

The Moustache caught a wrist, and in return received a small flying fist in his mouth.

"I'm not doing any better," he spit blood.

The Granite Man tried it once more. He took Janice by the waist and lifted her in the air. Her legs flailed wildly against his shins; he was tough enough to tolerate that pain, however. She beat her elbows against his rib cage and thought she was hitting stone. All the time she was screaming:

"Help! Let me go! Help!"

He tried to put his hand over her mouth, and that was all the advantage she needed. She sunk her teeth into his fingers, and he dropped her and bellowed his accusing complaint, "She bit me."

The Moustache took her by the thumb—a very painful

hold—spun her around, threw her back to the Granite Man.

"Can't you hold on to her? She keeps running away."

The Granite Man wrapped both powerful arms around her. "Help!" she screamed. "Police! Kidnapping."

"Gag her," he grunted.

The Moustache pulled out a handkerchief. There was a flicker of movement at the garden wall as if a huge surge of liquid mercury were pouring over it, powerfully, relentlessly, noiselessly.

The Phantom landed silently on his feet, started walking towards them with his uniquely light stride. The entire width of the pool separated them, and while he didn't try to raise his voice, his words carried clearly.

"The lady said let go. Put your hands in the air. Don't move. Freeze!"

The Moustache snatched at the gun that was in a fast-draw shoulder holster. He had no fear of this peculiarly garbed stranger. The masked man's guns were in buttoned holsters, therefore he couldn't clear a gun until there were a few bullets in him. And despite the size of this giant, the Moustache knew from experience there wasn't a man in this world who could keep breathing, much less moving, after he had the opportunity to pump a few bullets into him.

The Moustache made basic mistakes based upon fallacies. He never considered alternatives. It is true the Phantom's automatics were in buttoned holsters, yet that in no way prevented him from getting them in an almighty hurry. The gun was in his holster—no, it was in his hand. It was that quick.

To explore this phenomenon a bit further, we must backtrack a little. As was stated, the Moustache had a revolver in a shoulder holster that was designed especially for a quick draw. It was he who made the first determination to use a weapon. It was he who initiated the physical motion towards a gun.

Consider the time element. The Moustache is mentally prepared. He is in physical motion. His basic equipment is made expressly for speed. He has all the advantages—and he knows it. He also has the supreme advantage of confidence, in the awareness that he is going to win this battle. Therefore, he is not shaky, he isn't sweating, there is no flood of adrenalin in his bloodstream that could affect him adversely, he is both smooth and adroit. Most of all, he is mentally confident and precious seconds ahead of the Phantom.

Yet, even as the Moustache was in the very act of drawing, the Phantom had his own gun in hand. The Phantom fired. A billow of smoke, a lightning stroke, a thunderous clap, and a heavy-caliber bullet struck the Moustache's drawn revolver, exploding it out of his palm, numbing the hand, wrenching the wrist, almost breaking the thumb and forefinger.

For an instant the Moustache wasn't aware of what had happened to him, and when he did become aware, his brain shattered because he couldn't comprehend the causes of his own defeat. The one glaring fact was that he was defeated. The next logical step—and one he himself would have taken had he retained the advantage—would have been to pull the trigger again and then he would be dead.

He obeyed his primitive instinct for survival. He ran. He was a tough man, he had proven his toughness many times in hairy situations, yet he could no more have stopped running than he could have stopped breathing. It was in order to go on breathing that he ran.

The Phantom's gun was in his holster again, the holster was buttoned (and of the four eyewitnesses not one had seen him draw, including the man who was watching intently for him to draw, nor had any seen him holster his weapon—such was his speed) and the Phantom was in motion, taking those long, perfectly balanced strides.

There was no chance of the Phantom catching the Moustache. There was the width of the pool between them, and the Moustache, despite his bulk, was by no means slow. No chance at all—for an ordinary man.

The Phantom's cerebral synapses functioned faster than computers or transistors—in nanaseconds, millionths of a second. Thought and action were simultaneous. A few long strides to give him momentum, a mighty leap, a leap that took him high and arching towards the end of the springboard. He came down knees bent, letting his substantial weight bend the board, waiting for the precise instant that only a collegiate diving champion named Kit Walker (for Ghost Who Walks) could determine, the instant when the natural resiliency of the board and the coil springs of his power-laden legs overcame gravity and weight.

He rose. He soared. He flew high in the air, back arched, head up, legs straight, toes pointed, arms out and back like the wings of a swooping hawk. Gracefully gliding across the width of the pool, he moved with deceptive speed. As his body slowly tilted on the invisible fulcrum of physical laws, the masterly timing and perfection of his dive could be fully appreciated. The Man Who Cannot Die was not aiming for the water. His flight through air was going to end at an exact spot on land.

The racing Moustache could see nothing but an open gate in the garden wall. That was his sole objective, and in his panic he was blind to everything else. Therefore, he didn't see the Phantom coming toward him—the flying object moving downward to meet the fleeing object with exquisite precision—the Phantom's arms straight out before him, hands open to grab the Moustache's shoulders, body going into a ball to increase the velocity of his fall, knees bending, bending up to the body.

The Moustache was struck down by this human hammer. He was stopped in midstride as though both legs were jerked away from him. A man of strength and size, he was smashed to the flagstone patio by an inexorable force so far removed from his experience that he could no more comprehend it than could the fly the fly swatter.

The Moustache huffed hugely as the breath went out of his body as instantly as air leaves a pricked balloon. The Phantom performed a gymnast's roll, bounced to his feet, grabbed the Moustache, keeping the would-be murderer at arm's length. The Phantom's balled fist inscribed a short arc. Steel crashed against bone. The Moustache's head flicked back. His coat and shirt ripped in the Phantom's grip as he went hurtling backwards and splashed well out in the pool, unconscious before he touched the water.

The Granite Man's courage evaporated when he saw his partner on the road to defeat. He, too, tried to escape, choosing a path through the house that should be clear.

The Phantom, fresh from his contact with the Moustache's jaw, straightened his arm and hurled something. Only as it turned over and over in the air could one see it was his automatic pistol. No one had seen him draw, it was known his weapon was in his buttoned holster, and now it was in midair rapidly catching up to the Granite Man.

Again, let us backtrack to break down the Phantom's movements in order to comprehend his uncanny speed.

When he punched the Moustache, he was implanting on him the Bad Sign of the Phantom to mark him for all time. Although his fist didn't travel far, it was a powerful blow, delivered by shoulder and body. Recall that the Moustache's suit and shirt were ripped to shreds. This was accomplished with the same punch that had once knocked out a world champion, and while the Phantom could recover from it as fast as a tiger's stroke, there are newsreel films in existence that have been studied by professional boxers to see how the punch was delivered.

It is thrown from the right leg, foot planted solidly, body pivoting from the hips. It makes for one connection between ground and jaw, the delivery vehicle being bone and muscle. The knee does bend—though there have been arguments on this point—and the body does turn, as all have seen. It is the amazingly fast recovery to the "on guard" position that flabbergasts all viewers.

But we are interested in the moment of the body turning from hips and waist. Remember that the arm is flexed at the elbow. As the Phantom's body came around, the physical layout of the Helm estate allowed him to see the Granite Man attempting to escape.

The Phantom stopped the punch inches after he connected with his target—a fantastic feat much like catching a bullet in air. He then unflexed his elbow, straightening his arm. He must have unbuttoned his holster (this is the part no one can truthfully say they have seen) grabbed his automatic, flipped it in the air so he could catch it by the barrel, raised his arm, utilized his body's remaining turning motion, and thrown the automatic.

All this while finishing a punch.

The automatic was well thrown. The butt smashed on the Granite Man's skull, dropping him as fast as his partner had dropped. The Phantom strode swiftly, lifted the Granite Man, implanted the Skull Mark on his jaw, sat him against a wall. A few quick strides to the pool, and he hooked out the Moustache and sat him alongside Granite Man.

He was still alert. He glanced around to see if anything had been left undone, if there were reserves lurking behind bushes or waiting outside the garden wall.

Janice Helm blinked, not yet able to understand everything that had happened. All the action had occurred in something under four seconds. Only five seconds ago she had been struggling in the grip of the Granite Man. Then the weirdly dressed weight lifter bounced into the garden, said something, he was flying—shooting . . . I mean, hitting—no, throwing . . . well, anyway, these two professional thugs were stretched out cold. And here was this good-looking hunk of man. He had to be intelligent to put on a show like that, and if the rest of his assets came up to those he had displayed, it was a matter of "Girls, step to one side, he's mine, I saw him first, you don't want your eyes clawed out, do you, dears?"

A mechanical cough sounded, followed by the roar of a high-speed engine and the shriek of burning tires. The Phantom was an arrow from the bow, in high acceleration after his first leap. A blur going out the garden gate, he ran into a cloud of rising dust. Through it he could see a car racing away, lurching as the driver floored the accelerator. The Phantom stopped. He never wasted effort on a useless chase.

Janice was still in a state of shock when he walked back with his light stride. But still she could not help wondering who he was. Not somebody to be afraid of. On the contrary, he exuded enough confidence to give you confidence. A man who moved like he did, using the muscular power he did, had to be famous or important, or both. There was, however, that mask. Of course he could be a Robin Hood- type character.

He stood in front of her—goodness, he was even bigger than she thought—spoke his first words to her:

"They had a car waiting. The driver got away to report . . . somewhere."

"I seem to be safe now. Whoever are you?"

"Someone who helped."

"What platoon of marines always land just in time?"

"Platoon? Marines?"

"Only a platoon could act like that. And the marines always land just in time."

Ordinarily the Phantom would have been amused. Now he was preoccupied searching for the identity of the Granite Man and the Moustache. No wallets. Not a scrap of paper in their pockets. Even the suit labels had been cut off and their shirts bore no laundry marks. It all indicated they were highly professional thugs.

"Why," Janice asked, "did you throw your gun at him?"

"I dislike shooting—except when necessary." The Phantom took off the men's shoes and looked for manufacturer's marks. Nothing. Complete blanks. The shoes were new and the leather lining had no printing at all, not even size designation. Very professional. He stood.

"Who are these men?"

"I haven't the slightest idea. I don't even know who you are. Whether you're a good guy or a bad guy."

There were stifled sounds and chair legs knocking against the flagstone patio. Janice whirled, alarmed. "Good heavens! Gooley! I forgot. They tied her up."

Gooley was gagged, and securely bound in a chair, rocking it back and forth to draw attention to her predicament. She had seen everything that had happened. She had seen the Living Legend appear before her eyes, and while the Phantom was certainly no stranger to the Llongo, Gooley had spent most of her young life at the Helm estate in Mawitaan. As a village child, she had heard the stories whispered by the fire as it pressed back the blackness of the jungle; later, on vacations and holidays with her parents, she was told some tales of the Phantom, the Man Who Cannot Die. Now, here, in full view, in daylight, under a bright sun, she had seen the Ghost Who Walks perform his legendary feats. This was a story for the telling. Her village would chew on it for years.

The Phantom strode towards her, snapped in his fingers one of the binding cords, and the rest fell free. He was very gentle in removing her gag, stepped back to allow her to recover.

Janice knelt in front of her. "Are you all right, Gooley? Did they hurt you?"

"No, Miss Janice. I'm all right."

Then Gooley remembered her manners. She was in the presence of the Keeper of the Peace, the Law Giver, Ruler of the Jungle. She jumped to her feet, curtsied, spoke in Llongonese.

"Thank you, O Ghost Who Walks."

And he nodded. That was all. He nodded. Yet she knew he appreciated her thanks, that the deeds done here today were ordinary to him. In his calm, patient manner he waited to see if she had anything to say. It struck Gooley that the Man Who Cannot Die was four hundred years old. FOUR HUNDRED YEARS! Of experience. Battle, dealing with humans. He had seen everything, heard everything. Suddenly Gooley felt very young, childish, babyish before this man of awesome knowledge.

She ran into the house, not understanding why she ran, why she had to get away from the Keeper of the Peace. It was just that her mind couldn't encompass all he was and all he had been to her people. She needed time for mental readjustment.

"What was that all about" Janice wondered.

"She thanked me."

Janice had learned Llongonese as a youngster, forgotten most of it. But she still remembered simple phrases like thank you. "More than that!" She was unaccountably exasperated at this little mystery. "And her actions! I never saw Gooley bend her knee to any man. She seems to know you."

"It's possible."

Janice suddenly started shivering. She was white around the lips. Reaction was setting in.

The Phantom noticed. "Don't be afraid, Janice. There's nothing more to fear."

"I'm chilly." She pulled a towel over her shoulders. In a way her statement was true. Her blood pressure was dropping. Then it surged upwards as a realization—a false one —flooded her mind.

"You know my name! This was all planned. I see it now," she studied his costume, "you're a burglar. A cat burglar. The biggest cat I ever saw but still a crook. It was you and Gooley. Gooley told you to come here and rob. These two unconscious jokers must have overheard you planning the robbery. Well, I've got news for you—all of you—there's nothing here to steal. The laugh's on you," she laughed hysterically.

The Phantom recognized shock and took steps to halt it "Sit down!" his voice crackled like an electric arc. Indeed, there is a jungle saying, "The Phantom's command is sharper than a spear."

Janice promptly sat, and wondered why. One glare from between the slits of this man's mask, one word, and her knees had bent reflexively. There wasn't the slightest thought of disobeying him.

"Now stay there." The Phantom strode for the house.

With her usual volatile emotions (some men insisted it was emotional instability, but perhaps they were rejected suitors) Janice now examined this strangely dressed man. He was everything she had dreamed about—almost. He must be a crook. That, of course, would have to be changed, otherwise the rest was just fine. She sighed in resignation. She supposed it was up to her to do the changing. Once she turned on the charm, it shouldn't take more than a few weeks to change the man's life.

Inside, the Phantom picked up the phone, dialed Colonel Weeks's private number. "Colonel Weeks," he ordered, "send two men to the Helm estate. Arrest two criminals on charges of the attempted kidnapping of Miss Helm. Also for assault on Miss Helm and her maid, Gooley. Hold them and find out who they are."

As soon as Colonel Weeks acknowledged the orders, the Phantom hung up. He looked around the room. It was Victorian, with oil lamps and heavy furniture. He went to the window drapes, checked the cords. They were ponderous, over an inch thick, wrapped in velvet, and due to hanging loops and curlicues ending in tassels, were extensive in length. In order not to destroy the valance shielding the modem draw rods, he reached high, wrapped a rope around his left hand, snapped down with his right, and the rope parted, leaving only frayed strands at the ends. He wrapped it around his arm and went out to the patio again.

Janice—still sitting—grew tense and white about the mouth when she saw him. She thought the rope was for her. When the masked man bent and started tying the thugs, she felt an instant's relief, then in her emotional way started plotting again how she would change his life. Shouldn't take more than a week, if handled correctly.

"I phoned the Jungle Patrol," the Phantom said. "They'll pick up these men."

"You phoned—" Janice was startled. "But I thought—I mean—are you a cop or something?"

The Phantom's lips twitched in humor. "Or something."

Janice was in sudden good humor too. "Not plainclothes. Not like any clothes I ever saw."

The Phantom was in a hurry, came to the object of his visit. "Janice, were you ever at the Island of Dogs."

"Often as a kid. Swam there."

"Do you know your grandfather rented it?"

"Yes, that was a couple of years ago. I was in Europe then. Granddad didn't have much money, but he never touched the fund set aside for my education. He was a swinger, you know, the last of the old-style swingers, I guess. In fact, all the Helms were swingers. Anyway, he wrote that he had suddenly come into a lot of money by renting Dog's Island, doubled my allowance, and told me to come back here after I finished school. We were together only a few days when I woke up one morning and he was gone. There was a note that said he was off to Europe. I guess he was just waiting for me to get to Mawitaan. I mean, he must have thought Europe couldn't take both of us."

"Heard from him since?"

"No, but that's not unusual. Neither of us is much on writing letters. Should I worry?"

"He may be in trouble."

"Why? He wouldn't hurt a fly."

"Those men who came here—they brought a note?"

"Yes!" Janice picked it off the flagstones. "But you can see it's as phony as a three-dollar bill. Even my first name is misspelled. Good grief!—one's own grandfather. The one who brought you up. Misspelling your name."

"Why do you think those men came here, Janice?"

"Let's see," she ran a fingernail over her teeth. "A billionaire oil sheik saw me in Monte Carlo, my beauty drove him mad, he knew I'd never enter his harem, he hired an international gang of cutthroats to search the dark corners of the world. When they discovered me, they were to report to him, then he'd send after me his bearded tribesmen with bare scimitars thrust through their cummerbunds. I was never really in danger because John Wayne and you were secretly and passionately in love with me, and despite the rivalry between you, neither would—"

"I think those men were trying to kidnap you to the Island of Dogs."

Janice stayed in a flippant mood despite the Phantom's sobering words. "What would seafood packers want with me. I admit I'm quite a dish, but I'm hardly a cold fish."

"Did you ever meet these seafood packers?"

"No. Should I? Have I missed an experience?"

"They have an electric fence, assault rifles, mortars, anti-aircraft guns. Judge for yourself."

"Hey, I like them! When they say privacy, they really mean it. What are they protecting?"

"I'm going to find out."

"Heavy! Just let me change into my jeans."

"You're not going."

"Of course I am. I know every foot of the place."

"The situation's changed since you were last there. Do you have a picture of your grandfather?"

"Sure," she led the way to the house. "In here." She took an ornately framed photo off the grand piano, handed it to him.

The Phantom nodded. One glance and the face was permanently imprinted on his memory. "Another favor; don't tell the Jungle Patrol I've been here."

"That would be difficult. I don't know who you are," Janice pointed out in a broad hint. "I suppose I could ask Gooley. She seems to know you."

The Phantom was humored by her labored attempts to ascertain his identity. "Any answers Gooley gives will confuse you. You won't be able to integrate them into your experience." They were out on the patio now. She pointed to the Granite Man and the Moustache. "How am I going to explain these sleeping beauties to the Patrol."

"Janice," the Phantom's voice was sincere, "I'm confident you'll think of a marvelous explanation."

He leaped for the wall in amazing fashion, a single leap bringing his very substantial weight to the top. An effortless motion, and he paused on one knee and one foot.

Janice yelled after him. "When am I going to see you?"

"I don't think we'll be meeting again."

"Hey! You can't leave me flat. Not after we just met." The Phantom disappeared on the other side of the wall. There was only silence.

Janice looked after him, muttering, "We'll meet. You can bet your mask and costume on that."

CHAPTER 8

At Jungle Patrol Headquarters, Colonel Weeks cradled the phone softly. He had recognized the voice. There was no other like it. Riggs had found that out. Of course he always followed the orders of the Commander unquestioningly; but not blindly. He thought over the orders and carried them out with intelligence and dispatch—which was one of the reasons he was the highest-ranking officer in the Jungle Patrol.

He depressed the intercom switch on his desk, remembering which man had the alert duty. "Sergeant Doyle. You are to take Private Riggs and drive to the Helm estate in The Hills section—I believe Riggs knows the way. There you are to arrest two men on kidnapping and assault charges and return them here. One of you is to stay and guard the granddaughter, Janice Helm. Is that clear?"

"Yes, sir," Doyle answered, standing at his end. He was a big red-haired Irishman whose flattened nose proved that for many years he had been the Irish national heavyweight boxing champion. He was also a Fellow in Chemistry at Trinity College, and tutored mathematics on the side. In the Patrol he was considered to have a pretty wild sense of humor, which, in that group, was a reputation hard to win.

He walked into the barracks shouting, "Riggs! Riggs! Where are you, boy?" And when Riggs walked out of the lounge, Doyle smiled kindly on him.

"Five minutes, bucko, and then we're on our way. It's a desperate mission, so prepare yourself. I don't think you'll be coming back."

As soon as Doyle was out the door, Ned Kelly laughed. "The wind's up proper. Don't you mind Doyle, cobber. He's putting you on. Anything desperate and there'd be a weapons issue."

Stavros said, "I wouldn't keep him waiting."

The warning sufficed. Riggs prepared hurriedly, and was waiting outside the barracks when the sergeant drove by. Doyle's eyes flicked over him from head to toe, inspecting him. Then he said, "Get in, laddie."

The jeep cruised for The Hills section. Doyle asked, "Do you know where the Helm estate is?"

"Not exactly. I have the address."

"I got that much myself. A grand help you're going to be."

Riggs flushed. "I spoke to the granddaughter on the phone, that's all."

"Ah yes, the granddaughter," Doyle mused. "This desperate mission concerns her. It seems two gentlemen of ill repute tried to kidnap her. Rank amateurs they must be, for they flopped on the job. Now the Colonel wants them arrested and returned to Headquarters. Since they are such dangerous characters, I'll handle it alone."

Riggs turned in the seat. "Was Miss Helm hurt?"

"Not a bit of it, if my information is correct, and I have to admit it's pretty sketchy at this point. But it's you who'll be soothing any injured feelings or calming temper tantrums. Your duty, me boy, is to babysit for Miss Helm," Doyle roared with laughter.

Riggs nodded, keeping a straight face. "I see. Have you met Miss Helm?"

"Not to my knowledge," Doyle's whole body was heaving with laughter. "I'm sure the little darling will be most entertaining. She'll show you where she keeps her jacks, you can teach her tiddlywinks, both of you can read long passages of Mother Goose to each other. It's envious I am of you. It's a jolly time the two of you will be having."

"I hope so," Riggs commented emotionlessly.

Doyle reached for the radio, and still grinning, reported to Headquarters. "Sergeant Doyle logging in, accompanied by Private Riggs. Position is approximately one-half mile from the Helm estate. According to orders, Sergeant Doyle will apprehend two criminals and place them in Patrol custody. Private Riggs will bodyguard Miss Janice Helm. Will you give us a check please."

A minute's pause and then came the laconic answer, "Check."

"Any change in orders?"

"No. Carry on as planned."

Doyle parked outside the Helm place, walked through the gate and up the long walk to the main entrance.

Riggs asked him, "I suppose the radio call makes it official. I mean that I have to babysit."

"It does. Now that it is logged, couldn't change the assignment for the world. While you play with the kid, I'll heave the scoundrels in jail, then take my overheated body to the air-cooled canteen. The privilege of rank. Take heart, Riggs me boy. Someone will relieve you. Some time. In the distant or far future."

Riggs pulled down the corners of his mouth. "I've never met Miss Helm either, Sergeant, but if Colonel Weeks wants it, I'm willing to spend the rest of my enlistment guarding her."

"That's the proper spirit," Doyle clapped him on the back. "I'll see if I can't get you relieved. In a week or two." He rang the bell at the side of the huge double doors. They heard the unlocking of bolts, one door moved the length of a safety chain, and Gooley peered out the opening. Her eyes were still wide from recent fright.

"Jungle Patrol," Doyle held up his identification. "We were called?"

"Oh, yes," Gooley opened the door. "Come in, gentlemen. This way please," she showed them to a light and airy sunroom.

"Would you send for Miss Helm?" Doyle asked. "

Certainly," Gooley left them.

"Don't despair," Doyle gave Riggs a fleeting grin, "she may be a cute little tyke."

Janice came in from the patio, still dressed in the bikini, swaying indolently, one hand on her hip, the other carrying the towel. "Are you looking for me?" She glanced from one to the other.

Doyle gulped. "Mrs. Helm," he said hopefully.

"No. Miss Helm "

"You wouldn't have a daughter by chance?"

"Miss Helm, oaf. Are you here to take away my prize collection?"

"Yes ma'am. He is. That is, I . . . well . . ."

Janice stared curiously at him. "How did you get your stripes—bribery?"

"Ma'am! In the Patrol . . . I mean we wouldn't . . ."

"Can you talk without stumbling all over your tongue?" Janice switched her gaze to Riggs. "How does he ever give orders?"

Riggs's grin stretched from ear to ear. "He's in a state of confusion, Miss Helm. Something like the man who painted himself into a corner. He's here for two criminals reported on the premises."

"Oh, yes, them. They're by the swimming pool. I had better show you the way so the sergeant doesn't get lost."

Doyle muttered, "When I get you back in the barracks—"

"No rush, Sergeant," Riggs was all condescension. "In a week. Or two. Some time. In the far future. I think that's what you said. I can wait."

"I've got the peculiar feeling I've been plotted against."

"Or been hoisted on your own petard? Hey!" Riggs stopped suddenly. "Look at those two!"

Doyle stopped, eyed them with professional interest "Those are big boys. Who knocked them out and tied them up?"

Janice put a finger to her mouth coquettishly. "I did. My hand-to-hand combat techniques were a little rusty, but they came back. Throat slash, solar plexus stab, leg sweep, ankle trip, elbow punch. You know, the usual things."

"The usual?" Doyle took off his helmet and scratched his red hair. "Oh yeah. Of course." He knelt by them and studied them as he once studied opponents in the ring.

"These are very rugged types." He examined their hands. "Professionals, by their callouses. They're still out cold and it's been more than a half hour since you called. Excuse me, Miss Helm, but it's hard to believe you could do all this."

"A lot of people make that mistake," she passed the matter off with a casual wave.

Doyle pushed the Granite Man's head back to inspect the jaw more closely. "There's some sort of a mark here. Where a good right cross would land. Like . . . like a skull mark. Couldn't be an identification or tattoo. These professionals have them removed Did you hit them with anything, Miss Helm?"

"Just my fist."

"That doesn't explain how the skull mark got there."

"Phantom," Gooley said from the sidelines. "Ghost Who Walks."

"What did you say?"

Janice interrupted quickly. "Girl talk. Between us girls."

"Oh. Any idea what these men wanted?"

"Ransom, I guess. They sure didn't come here for a polite introduction."

"Yes. Well . . . very mysterious, this affair. I'll be borrowing Riggs for a minute to help me get these sides of beef into the jeep, then he's yours."

"Mine! What am I going to do with him?"

"Nothing. I hope. Orders from the Colonel, miss. He's to be your bodyguard."

"The last thing I need is a bodyguard."

"After observing the condition of these two that'd be my opinion, but orders are orders. Then there's always the possibility these sleeping beasties have friends."

Riggs already had the Granite Man under his shoulders. Doyle grabbed his feet and they carried him to the jeep. After dumping him in the back seat, Doyle asked, "Wouldn't be trying to get rid of me, would you, bucko?"

"Sergeant, you distinctly said I was to give you a hand. I interpreted that as an order."

"Well, well, now it's a stickler for the rules you are."

"I didn't think you'd want it any other way. Sergeant."

They piled the Moustache next to the Granite Man and again Doyle paused. "It would be just bending a rule a bit if you drove these babies back to Headquarters."

"Sergeant, you logged over the radio the fact that I was to stay on here as Miss Helm's bodyguard. If we switched assignments, it would confuse the duty roster. The Colonel would be sure to find out. As you yourself said, orders are orders. I'm content to do my duty and babysit with Miss Helm."

"Aye, laddie, you'll go far. As a matter of fact," Doyle held up a fist like a battering ram, and admired it, turning it to and fro, "I'm tempted to send you far."

Riggs played it straight—which was most aggravating. "You're in command on this mission. I think you mentioned the privilege of rank."

"Thanks for reminding me. I'll pray for you. That at the physical-training periods we step into the ring together." Doyle got behind the wheel. Janice came up.

"Oh, Sergeant," Riggs reminded him in calm tones, "will you see to the supply of jacks and Mother Goose books."

Tires squealed and the scent of burning rubber was left behind as the jeep roared away.

"What was that all about?" Janice demanded.

"Er . . . a private joke between us."

Janice led the way back inside the house. "I'll accept the answer—for now. Are you going to be staying here?"

"The Colonel says you need a bodyguard."

Janice stopped and turned directly in his path. "Do you think I need a bodyguard?"

Riggs flushed. She was standing very close to him. Against him, actually. "Ah . . . hmmm . . . I'm a private. I'm not supposed to think."

Janice turned, satisfied. Her effect on men was still in good working condition. "All right, Private John Riggs. Sit down and wait."

"Er . . . I'm supposed to follow you everywhere."

"Not into my dressing room," she slammed the door in his

face, and giggled. He was a nice-looking young man, but his problem was that he was so young, so naive.

"Gooley," she shouted. "I'm going to take a shower now. Lay out something nice for me to wear. Simple but elegant. Meanwhile, tell me about the masked man. Phantom, I think you called him."

"Yes, miss," Gooley almost did another curtsy. Quite evidently she held this Phantom in awe. "Ghost Who Walks. He is Ruler of the Jungle, Keeper of the Peace. He is stronger than ten tigers, has the wisdom of the ages for he is four hundred years old."

Janice turned on hot water, added cold to it. "That's nonsense, Gooley. Surely you don't believe it. You're educated. I mean, just look at him. He can't be four hundred years old. He's young."

"I know what I know. Miss Janice. He's the Man Who Cannot Die."

"You'd better start again. He's called the Phantom, right?"

"Yes. All the jungle knows him."

"And he's four hundred years old. He never ages?"

"That is what the jungle knows. We have men in the jungle who are ancient, may be one hundred years old. They say when they were young, Phantom was young."

"He certainly didn't act old today."

"No, Miss Janice. He put his bad sign on those bad men, marked them permanently. You saw."

"I saw. I'm just having a difficult time believing."

She thought about him. He was strong, quiet, mysterious, pleasing to the eye like a black panther which, at the same time, you know is very dangerous. He attracts and yet repels. But there was certainly nothing repelling about him. *Au contraire, très beau.* He said they'd never meet again, but he didn't know Janice Helm very well; not at all, in fact.

"Gooley. He's not a crook, is he?"

"Oh no, Miss Janice. He's a good man. You've never known such a good man. He puts his good sign on people and villages and places, and they are protected from all evil. I've seen it. No one would dare harm what Phantom protects."

"Then everyone fears him?"

"No. Everyone loves him."

"Hmm. That does make a difference. A lot of difference."

She slipped into a simple black dress made by one of the famous couturiers, accented it with a necklace of pearls. She knew she looked magnificently beautiful and didn't mind saying so. How could a man resist her? Any man? This nonsense about his being four hundred years old was . . . plain ridiculous on the face of it. Suppose he was married—when? Back in the 1500s sometime. Then his wife would be four hundred years old too, and ugh! what a hag after all that time. Yet his finely modeled face was unlined.

"Gooley," she chased after her to the kitchen, "is the Phantom married?"

"I never heard," Gooley retreated a step as though it was a subject she didn't want to touch, "I don't think he is. And don't you be a silly girl with silly ideas about marrying him," she grew stern. "Phantom is Ruler of the Jungle, Miss Janice. He never dies. He's not like . . . he's not for ordinary folk."

"Who says I'm ordinary?"

"Don't get your hopes up. Phantom can be called in times of danger, and he comes. But if he doesn't want you to see him, you never see him."

"I'm in danger, Gooley."

"He knows. He was here. He kept you from harm. I tell you the jungle truth, Miss Janice, you never meet him again unless he wills it."

Janice smiled sweetly, and thought to herself. That's what you think, Gooley—and that's what Mr. Phantom thinks, but it's not what Janice Helm thinks.

Colonel Weeks went outside his office when he heard Doyle's jeep draw up. Doyle saluted smartly, and since the Colonel was uncovered, he acknowledged Doyle with a signal of his pipe stem. He studied the two trussed men in the back, then asked the natural question, "Are they alive?"

"Yes, sir. Unconscious."

"Hmmm," he searched for the pulses in their necks. "Shallow breathing. Really out cold. Did you and Riggs do this?"

"No, sir! We found them in that condition. The curtain ropes were already on them. The girl said she did it."

"What is she, a lady wrestler?"

"More like a movie starlet. She says she's trained in hand-to-hand. I've seen some women karate experts. They're all smooth-muscled like a sleek house cat. This girl is in good shape—great shape," he added, his blue Irish eyes twinkling, "but she doesn't appear physically to have undergone extensive combat training."

"Then she must have had help. These men weigh well over two hundred pounds apiece. They look like they were; in the way of an elephant stampede. Any evidence of a desperate struggle?"

Doyle had marshaled his facts. "The one with the moustache was evidently knocked in the pool. His clothes are wet and there was a trail of water on the patio leading to where he had been trussed up like a Christmas goose. The very large ugly fellow has a lump on his head the size of an egg."

There was a shift in the sunlight, and the Colonel noticed the marks on their jaws. Skulls! It explained a lot. "All right, Doyle," he puffed on his briar. "Take them to the infirmary, have them patched up. Notify me when they come around."

He walked back to his office, doing a good deal of heavy thinking. The skull mark was the sign of the Phantom. The Commander had called him to pick up the two men at Janice Helm's place. He drew the logical conclusion—which he had drawn before— that the Phantom and the unknown Commander were one and the same. This piece of logical reasoning did him little good because the next question was—who is the Phantom? Over the course of the years, he had actually seen the masked man with his own eyes, but that did little to reveal his identity. With all the investigative facilities at his command, he had never been able to solve the greatest mystery of all—Phantom!

Yet, everywhere he turned there was evidence of the works of this remarkable man. And he was remarkable—if he were a mortal man like the rest of us. For instance, there had been the conversation with the Landons regarding the boy's research into the mark of the skull. All forensic scientists swore under oath no human could apply that mark permanently to the jaw of a man. It took a pile driver's stroke. Yet Randolph Weeks had seen with his own eyes hundreds of criminals bearing the brand that the jungle people called, and rightly so, the Bad Sign.

A more recent occurrence involved a time-distance relationship. Riggs had been interviewed by the Commander in the Jungle of Night. By his own testimony he had floored the jeep's gas pedal racing back. Yet shortly after he arrived at Headquarters, the Commander had phoned from the Helm estate instructing that the two kidnappers be picked up.

The Jungle of Night was in one direction, the Helm estate in the opposite direction, with Headquarters and Mawitaan approximately on a line between. How could the Commander have traveled so quickly? By helicopter? Radar would have picked him up, and furthermore, no helicopter could penetrate the Jungle of Night. Neither could he have come by road—not in the outlandish garb of the Phantom. There was the possibility of traveling cross-country—not on foot of course—except what steed could maintain the necessary pace? Randolph Weeks had heard the jungle legend of the great white stallion that crashed like thunder and galloped like the wind, followed by a monstrous wolf, and he filed the legend under the category of all good stories— imagination. Now he was beginning to have doubts regarding his own judgment. Perhaps the legends were true. Perhaps, as Officer in Charge of the Jungle Patrol, it was well to maintain a healthy skepticism.

The buzz of the intercom disturbed his musings. It was Doyle.

"Sir, Dr. Garrett has patched up our guests. They're in the outer office. He'd like to talk to you."

"Very well. Send them in."

Dr. Garrett wore the traditional white jacket of his profession, and he further fulfilled the common ideas concerning doctors by wearing glasses, having graying hair, and a white moustache. There he parted with the usual concepts. He was a specialist in two fields, surgery and tropical medicine, and could have made a fortune in any capital of the world as a surgeon. Indeed, he was famous in medical circles for some of his radical innovations, but he preferred to practice his skills where they were needed most, in the jungle and the Jungle Patrol.

The two thugs he ushered in front of him had been calmed considerably, didn't look so tough anymore. They were patched and bandaged, and like all of their kind were quite subdued when in the presence of law officers.

Dr. Garrett asked the question that was uppermost in his mind. "Randolph, did your boys work them over with baseball bats?"

"No. Never laid a violent hand on them."

"Only their rugged physiques kept them from real harm. They're hoods, of course. Have numerous bullet and knife and contusion scars. I've only seen their like on criminals. Who roughed them up?"

Colonel Weeks exhaled a smoke cloud, spoke airily, "The best information I have is that a girl did it."

"Incredible! She must be a football team. These two are real toughs. Some of their injuries are extremely painful, but I haven't gotten an 'ouch' out of them, much less a word. I'd like to see the girl who is a one-man—no, that's the wrong word—a one-girl army. Women's Lib indeed! This is carrying it to the extreme. My best advice to you, Randolph, is to sign her up for the Patrol. I'd like to see her."

"From the description I've received, I think you'd be surprised."

"Not likely. I've seen too much in this life. Oh, one thing I haven't seen before. They have identical marks on their jaws. Very odd. Shaped like a skull. They're not tattoos. I've used ether, carbon tet, the usual dissolvers and some pretty exotic ones. Nothing takes them off."

"Don't try. I've seen the marks before. They're permanent. Now if you'll leave us alone, Doc."

Once the door closed, Colonel Weeks's amiable manner changed. His face hardened. His eyes glared. His voice became raspish, snappish, and none of it was an act. He detested these types of human animals.

"You two have a lot to answer for. Abduction and assault are the least of it. We can do this the hard way or the easy way, take your choice. First thing we'll find out are your names. Give them to me."

The two thugs glared at him.

Colonel Weeks seated himself behind his desk. "I can wait. So can you. Standing. The report on your fingerprints should come in soon. We'll find out who you are then." He pulled an accumulation of papers close to him and started signing them.

"I should inform you that eventually you'll be turned over to the Mawitaan authorities, and with the evidence we have, I don't think there's any doubt of a conviction. The Mawitaan Penitentiary is no luxury resort. Mayor Togando and Chief of Police Togando don't believe in pampering criminals who have committed crimes of violence. Their prescription is hard labor, and those who refuse to work don't eat. It's amazing how effective that is despite all the sociological theories to the contrary. Strong men like you will be set appropriate tasks. Since life sentences in this country mean you spend your life in prison, you'll be old and gray before you get any rest."

He read quickly through a series of reports, letting his last statement sink in. At what his experience told him was the proper psychological moment, he said, "Of course the Jungle Patrol has the authority to return you to your native country upon a guarantee you'll be tried and judged there. That is, if we discover where you're from."

The two thugs stared straight ahead.

Randolph Weeks went on with his work, not looking at them. "Perhaps you don't speak English." He pressed the intercom switch, and summoned a group of his multilingual talents.

For three hours Jungle Patrolmen speaking most of the common languages of the world paraded in and out of Weeks's office. All of them admitted to failure—if not linguistic failure, then the inability to get the two thugs to answer to any language, including their native tongue. When their fingerprint records were returned with the statement, there was no criminal record on them. Randolph Weeks shrugged and reached for the phone. The crimes had been committed in Mawitaan jurisdiction, let Police Chief Togando take it from there.

A knock on the door interrupted him. Sergeant Doyle opened it. "Sir, there's an attorney here to see you, a Lionel Crabbe."

"Oh? I'll see him in the outer office."

Colonel Weeks had his usual feeling of distaste for the lawyer. He had the strong sensation he was dealing with a devious man.

"Yes?" he queried, refusing to say more, making Crabbe

commit himself.

The sour-looking Crabbe said, "I believe you have two men here?"

"I have a large number of men here." Colonel Weeks answer was intentionally evasive. He was surprised that Crabbe knew the thugs had been arrested, and the best way to gain information from his sort was to refuse to give any.

"The two men I'm referring to were arrested by the Patrol at the Helm estate."

"Are you representing Major Helm in this matter?"

"No. I'm representing them."

"Oh. You know them?"

"Hardly. I've never seen them."

"Then how can you represent them?"

"I received instructions by phone. I understand they're being held for a bailable offense."

"You were telephoned? By whom?"

"Their employer."

"And who is their employer?"

"You're being deliberately obstructive, Colonel."

"I always cooperate—with those who cooperate with me."

"I understand. Very well then, they work for the seafood packers on the Island of Dogs."

Colonel Weeks smiled to himself. He had suspected it. He lit his pipe to hide the expression of satisfaction on his face and spoke through the smoke. "They come from there to abduct Miss Helm?"

"No! It was all a stupid mistake. They had a message from her grandfather, and they don't speak English—"

"Nor apparently any other language. What is their native tongue?"

"I don't know. It's a multinational company. As I was explaining, they had this message, and Miss Helm misunderstood their intentions, became hysterical, and sent for you."

"That's not quite correct. However, I am curious as to how you know the sequence of actions without ever talking to the men."

"Colonel, you have no other choice but to drop the kidnapping charge. I've explained the unfortunate circumstances to you, and I can explain them to a magistrate. As to any assault charges pending against them. I'm prepared to post bail."

"Very interesting, Mr. Crabbe. I'll release them in the custody of the court. Of course if they don't appear for trial, I'll be obliged to go to the Island of Dogs and search for them."

"I'm sure you'll be welcomed," Lionel Crabbe said icily.

With Janice Helm, action followed thought in an instant. She wanted to see the marvelous masked man again and thought she knew how to do it. All events seemed to revolve around the Island of Dogs; therefore, go there.

She proceeded through the house. Private Riggs jumped out of a chair. "Come along, bodyguard," she motioned to him.

He didn't hear her. He was stunned. This was the first time he had seen her rigged out in a dress, and, if possible, she was more beautiful than in a bikini. As she trotted out the front door, he realized that she was leaving, that he was supposed to be with her, and he felt very foolish as he ran after her.

"Where are we going?"

"For a ride," she kept up the fast pace, heading towards the convertible parked in the driveway.

"It's getting dark. I'm not sure we should."

"What? Drive in the dark?"

"I mean leave the premises."

"I'm leaving," she slid into the driver's seat, "you can stay if you want."

"Let me phone Headquarters first."

"Go ahead. You don't have to ask my permission." She started the engine.

He jumped into the passenger seat; she engaged the gears and took off at a speed that snapped his neck.

"At least tell me where we're going, Miss Helm," he shouted over the blast of wind.

"Call me, Janice. And don't be a party-pooper, Riggs. Getting there is half the fun."

"Where?" Mawitaan flashed past his eyes like a runaway movie film.

She didn't bother answering, and in a few minutes braked shrilly on one of the docks. Snapping the keys out of the car, she strode quickly towards the end of the pier. A lean racy speedboat was tied up there.

"Isn't that a kick?" she grinned at it.

"Great," Riggs agreed. "Where is it supposed to take us?"

"The Island of Dogs."

"Janice! You can't go there."

"Who says? My grandfather owns it."

"It's off limits. For the Patrol, I mean."

"That's your problem." She descended the ladder on the pier to a floating platform, stepped into the boat.

Riggs wiped sweat off his upper lip. He had always been

certain of what he should do in his life and now . . . good grief! This girl did everything that was contrary to his nature. Like all uncertain men, he temporized.

"I'll phone Headquarters and get orders."

"Go ahead. The phone's at the other end of the pier," she uncleated the stern line and started working on the bow.

John Riggs suddenly realized she was leaving whether he was in the boat or not. He decided to obey orders by accompanying her, come what may. He bounded down the ladder as Janice was starting the engine, made a flying leap for the boat as it pulled away, and barely made the seat.

"Janice," he tried to change her mind. "Can you find the Island of Dogs?"

"Sure. It's still there, isn't it?"

"I mean in the dark."

"Why not? I've been there plenty of times."

"That doesn't mean you can find it now," the prow of the boat was lifting from acceleration. "I'm not sure I should let you go."

"Riggs, you've very nice and I like you, but any time you think you can order me around is the time you leave. The exit is over the side."

John Riggs came to the rational conclusion that argument was futile.

Night fog drifted over the Mawitaan waterfront, shielding the decrepit area with a merciful blanket. The Phantom strolled slowly through the white mist. Devil at his heels. If the ferocious "dog" were not enough to make the cutthroats lurking in doorways and behind pilings think twice, then the size of the man was.

He was wearing his Kit Walker costume comprising a soft-crowned hat with brim pulled down, dark glasses, long trench coat, and trousers. It was an effective disguise that allowed him to move through the normal world without causing too much curiosity. Walking out on a pier whose planks were soft from weather and the grime of years, he stopped to inspect a dilapidated shack where the light shone through warped boards. On the gray shingled roof that wasn't quite weatherproof was a sign advertising, "Boats for Rent." According to the shaky painted script at the bottom, Joe Morgan was the proprietor.

The Phantom knocked twice. The door was a lot more solid than a cursory glance would have indicated, and the big fist of the Phantom made it boom. Immediately a raspy voice sounded from inside:

"Go away. Come back in the morning."

The steel knuckles of the Phantom descended three times, demanding entrance. The shack shook. Dirt rained from the pier and sprinkled the oily waters below. Drunks shifted uneasily in their sleep.

Joe Morgan cursed, lunged for the door to deal with whomever was annoying him. He was big, burly, and a lifetime at sea had taught him to deal with problems immediately. His reputation for toughness was justly earned by punching first and inquiring afterwards. Now he was going to teach a lesson to this moron who annoyed him by pounding on his door with a hammer.

Jerking open the door, he stopped his forward motion cold and gulped at the figure filling the entrance. The imposing shadow spoke in a voice that could come only from a massive chest.

"I want to rent a boat."

Joe Morgan had seen overwhelmingly large men before — indeed, he was of an impressive size himself—and he had learned that stature alone doesn't indicate strength.

"Whatd'ya want?" he growled.

"I want to rent a boat."

"Not after dark. I told ya. Come back tomorrow," he slammed the door.

Except the door didn't close more than halfway. Something solid was stopping it. Morgan pushed again, angry, using all his muscle, almost biting his cigar stub in half with effort, and it still didn't move a millimeter. He looked down, expecting to see the stranger's foot wedged in the jamb, and was going to stomp on it—except no foot was there. Raising his eyes, he could see by the interior lights that the stranger had his hand against the door. Twice Morgan had pushed with force, and neither the arm nor the man had quivered. That was pure strength.

The arm started straightening; the door opened more, and Morgan, with his shoulder still against it, skidded along the floor.

"Now," the stranger said calmly.

As the door opened more fully, Morgan kept skidding. A monstrous wolf slid in and walked to one side and sat down. The mere act of sitting was a threat. There was hell-fire in the beast's green eyes, and the lips curled back from white fangs that gleamed. Kit Walker pushed the door open without the slightest strain. Joe Morgan decided on using a line of tactful bluff.

"Whatd'ya mean barging in here?"

"I don't like doors slammed in my face."

"That don't change my policy none. I still don't rent boats after dark. That'd be risky business in these parts, and old Mrs. Morgan didn't raise no fool."

"I'll pay well."

"No fee's enough to cover the cost of my boats."

"You'll act as pilot—and return with the boat."

Morgan was relieved he didn't have to argue with this obdurate man anymore. "Well now, that changes the complexion of things, don't it?"

"I'm told you know these waters as well as any man. Can we make the Island of Dogs before dawn?"

"Easy. An hour or less in my power boat."

"Sailboat. Don't ask the reason why."

"Sail, eh," Morgan removed the cigar stub from his mouth, pushed his nautical cap back on his head, and scratched his hairy chest through the holes of his grimy T- shirt. "Calm sea tonight," he thought aloud. "The air is moving and should be better out beyond the point Aye, we'll make it and with time to spare."

"Then let's leave."

"Just collect some gear. If that wolf's going, keep him away from me. He stares at me like I was his next meal."

"He won't harm you—as long as you tend to your job." They got in a rowboat, and Morgan manned the oars, rowing to a mooring where a sailboat was tied up.

"We'll take the sloop." He took sails out of a canvas sack and started bending them on. "She's light and quick."

The Phantom waited patiently, staying out of the way. "Getting us there is your business."

"Aye," Joe Morgan took the tiller and the sloop glided away from the mooring, "it'd be a lot quicker in a power boat."

They were silent until they reached the point where the wind quickened, and Morgan put her on a long reach. Then he cleared his throat, "None of my business, but what's on that island it's so important you have to get there tonight?"

"You're right. It is none of your business."

In the bow Devil shifted uneasily. Morgan, realizing that he had never had two more dangerous passengers, decided to shut his mouth and tend to sailing.

Janice Helm turned off the engine and drifted in a patch of fog, the speedboat rocking in the waves. Riggs twisted in the seat to face her.

"What's the matter? Are we lost?"

"If you say 'I told you so,' I'll toss you overboard. Now be quiet I'm trying to listen for breakers."

"You won't hear them. When I came out by helicopter, we followed approximately the same route, and we were on a different compass heading. A little elementary trigonometry proves you're way off course."

"Good grief!" Janice exclaimed. "I have a navigation aid aboard."

"I am trying to help," Riggs was conciliatory. "I thought you knew your way, or I would have said something before this."

Janice looked at him. "What other annoying habits do you have beside being cocksure of everything?"

"My major one seems to be annoying you. It's undeserved. You're a stubborn mule, you know."

"What!" Janice stood, bracing herself against the rolling of the boat.

"That's right. You're the type who gets in trouble, then expects other people to get you out of it"

"Listen, buster, I've been getting myself out of trouble since I tripped my first boy in ballet class. I'd rather have a shark in the boat than you."

"From those fins circling the boat, you might. Sit down, make a ninety-degree turn, run for five minutes, then turn off the engine again. At least we'll be getting nearer the Island of Dogs instead of further away."

Janice sat down, gunned the engine, spoke through thinned lips. "I hope we're hopelessly lost. I want to watch you suffer from thirst, starvation, fever, everything that happens to those lost at sea."

"The same thing will happen to you," Riggs pointed out quite reasonably.

"No it won't. Nothing happens to me—unless I make it happen."

"Besides, we're not really lost at sea. We're still in the Bight of Bangalla. Come morning, there'll be a lot of traffic."

Janice restrained herself from screaming. "If you make one more disgusting display of knowledge, I'll turn the boat over and leave a note saying you murdered me. Now shut up!"

Since they are going in the right direction, Riggs didn't bother mentioning it was her intemperate nature that had gotten them into this predicament. A beautiful girl, undoubtedly. She needed a man who'd treat her firmly. He could be that man . . . but he was dreaming a foolish dream. She hated him.

Joe Morgan had left the fog behind. He pointed straight over the bow to where there was a white line of breakers in the dark sea.

"Dead on," he mouthed as he treated himself to a new cigar. "There she is. Dog Island. Another half mile and I'll drop you on the beach. Won't even get your feet wet."

"This is as far as you go, Morgan. I'll swim from here."

"Swim!" Morgan was startled at the idea. "Hey, mister, these are shark waters. And I mean bad. You couldn't make a hundred yards, much less a half mile."

The passenger, now in the bow, was silent. Joe Morgan peered into the darkness and saw a black shadow outlined against the brighter night sky. Was this guy going skinny-dipping? No, there was something around his waist. Like holsters, maybe.

The figure threw a bundle of clothes at him. The deep voice sounded: "Keep these at your place. I'll pick them up later. Your fee's in the trench coat pocket."

As Morgan searched for the money, he asked, "Even if you do make it, how ya gonna get back from the island?"

He had been brought up in the tradition of the sea—passengers come first.

"Not your worry," was the calm answer. "Turn about. Go back to Mawitaan."

"I can lay off here waiting."

"No! Start back. Now!"

Joe's searching fingers found the money. He held it to the faint light cast by the binnacle. "Hey! This is too much."

"Keep it. Come on, Devil."

There were two distinct splashes, and Joe Morgan was alone.

CHAPTER 9

The Phantom swam with slow powerful strokes for the island with Devil at his side. He was as noiseless as the sharks that were cruising at a distance and didn't know there was a possible meal in the water. But the presence of sharks wasn't the reason for Phantom's silent swimming. He strongly suspected there was a twenty-four-hour watch on the island, and he had every intention of avoiding it.

As he felt bottom under him, he stopped swimming and let the waves carry him ashore. Above the water line, foam licking his feet, he laid listening, face down so as to prevent starlight reflections from shining off his eyes and the ridges of his face. Devil crouched and cocked his ears in imitation of his master.

The loud, random thumps and bangs of heavy machinery came to him, not the regular beating sounds that could be expected from a factory processing fish on an assembly-line basis. He listened below the level of this noise for such little sounds as a shoe crunching against sand or the scrape of a leather sole on rock.

Nothing. Perhaps they were relying on radar, thermo-sensors, infrared radiation, the more exotic warning devices. That gave the Phantom grim amusement. There was no better guard in the world than a trained man on the alert. Reliance on technology produced laziness in men. But a well-trained man who used technology as an extension of his own senses, that man was the most dangerous man on the face of the earth.

He backed into the waves again, slid through the foam to the rocky pile on the right of the beach. Carefully he eased out of the water, Devil following, hunkering down without being told. The Phantom used the rocks jutting out of the beach as protection, aware they'd give a scatter reflection on a radar screen and he'd be lost in the pattern.

The sand was soft all the way to the fence. "Stay away, Devil," he whispered, and started digging a trench. In a few minutes, he had a sense of satisfaction—the fence didn't go down far into the sand. They—the mysterious seafood packers—had made a basic mistake. They thought the electric charge through the fence was a good enough first line of defense. If the Phantom had been alone, he would have leaped over the wire; hampered by Devil's inheritance to leap for distance rather than height, he had to tunnel under. If all "their" defenses were as carelessly built as this, he'd have little trouble. Only a determined man could stop a determined man, and when the Phantom wanted to do something, there was nothing in this world that could stop him. Momentarily, perhaps, but not for long.

The passage was soon dug, and he wiggled his mighty frame under. Next came Devil, following his master's advice: "Come on, boy. Stay down. Down. Come on."

The Phantom didn't close the trench, as many would have done. He wanted it to attract attention. To further confuse the issue, he took Devil's paws and pressed them in the sandy loam where they made deep imprints.

"Let them think there's at least one dog on the Island of Dogs. Now come on, boy, we'll disappear."

Both of them quickly and silently climbed the upthrust of rock that formed the rim of the bowl-shaped island. Nearing the top, he edged around boulders, working towards a position where the central part of the bowl would be spread before him. The events of the past few days, the experience of the Landons and the Llongo Peace Delegation, and the helicopter fly-over by Private Riggs had prepared him for the sight of an industrial complex. He was expecting it. Riggs had told him about the cranes and towers and piers. The time interval since indicated there would be more construction. Besides, the Phantom was a veteran of bizarre sights, of the unusual, the horrible.

Yet, as he stared over the rim, even he was startled by what he saw.

Janice Helm shut off the engine. At least they were out of the fog now, although she hated to admit it was because of the directions given by Patrolman John Riggs. He was obnoxious and that was the end of it. One of those men who obeyed the rules and had an answer for everything. Good grief! He was too stiff to have fun, too rigid to unbend.

The engine shuddered into silence. They both heard the pounding of surf off to the right at the same time. Janice reached for the key again. Riggs covered her hand with his hand.

"Be careful. They don't appreciate strangers. They fired an anti-aircraft gun at me."

"I think they showed uncommon good sense."

"I don't care what you think, Janice. As long as I'm assigned to guard you, I'll guard you. Make a careful approach. If you intend to blunder ahead. I'll have to take control of the boat."

"My boat to my island?"

"That's right." He wore his determined look again.

Janice kicked the engine to life. While there was no way of muting such a powerful motor, she did make a slow and relatively quiet approach, holding the craft down to the lowest possible speed. Off to the right of the beach there was a wave-cut channel in the rocks, and at the end was a sheltered cove.

Once landed, she'd have to get rid of Riggs. Then she'd find the Phantom. Such a romantic character! A little changing and he'd be perfect. What would he look like without the mask?

Under bright lights, the Island of Dogs was a beehive of activity. The ship was still off loading. Flatcars, covered with tarpaulins, were lined end to end on the railroad tracks. Heavily loaded trucks came off the pier and trundled to various destinations. Men in cranes lifted steel beams, and more men crawled over partially completed towers and welded them in place. Everywhere were piles of discarded lumber and heaps of earth taller than some of the buildings.

Whatever was being constructed on this island was still in an unfinished state but was being rushed to completion. The Phantom came down out of the rocks like a stalking animal intent on his prey. Cautiously he moved along the rear of a concrete house, dashed into a shadow and bellied down. Devil was still by his side. There was no fear of his being seen. And yet a dispute could be made as to whether the wolf or the Phantom was better at making an invisible approach.

Armed sentries patrolled between the lighted areas and sectors of darkness. The Phantom slipped between them, flitting from shadow to shadow, always aiming in the direction of the flatcars. He wanted to see what was so important that it had to be covered. Once near the railroad tracks, he dropped down behind the raised side that was in shadow, and made rapid progress. He was getting nearer, nearer to the stationary train. Now the last car was so close he could almost touch it. Quick as an eye blink, he went over the track, scrambled along the ties, and was under the last car. Crawling, he emerged between two of the flatbeds and stood alongside a coupling.

The tarp was lashed down with cord through grommets. He broke the cord and all the grommets unstitched, allowing the tarp to be raised. A wide flare of metal nozzles faced the Phantom. He frowned, not immediately identifying them.

Going around to the side of the car, he lifted the tarpaulin there. A wing was near the base of a long cylinder, and the Phantom's jaw muscles bulged in anger as he realized what he was looking at, what was the secret of the Island of Dogs.

He was looking at a short-range atomic missile. The Island of Dogs was a missile site. A secret missile base. It came under no authority except the nominal authority of Major Matthew Helm— who had believed he was leasing the place to seafood packers, not to a major participant in the Cold War. In just a short time, the site would be finished, and then it would be a major pawn on the international chessboard.

He passed concrete silos dug deep into the bedrock of the island. Rockets from these could carry hydrogen warheads. The towers were for an obvious purpose; the Big Birds would fly from them.

The sentries wore civilian clothes and carried military assault rifles. They were soldiers in everything but their dress. Even the construction men were from construction battalions. The tacticians would naturally be soldiers. There would be few civilians, only highly qualified engineers and other personnel that could not be filled by armed forces— and they would be under the command of the military.

So far there were about one thousand men counted on the island—the estimate of Riggs, the helicopter pilot MacGregor, and the Phantom himself—and there was barracks space for five thousand. The conclusion was that more were coming and that when this last party came, the secret base would be fully manned, and from here they could control by threat of force all of Africa and Asia.

It was bad politics but brilliant military strategy. An accomplished fact could be argued about, not removed.

The Phantom had to remove the base. How was a question not even he could answer. Yet.

Well over to one side of the area was a wooden building looking much like a tool-shed. It was inferior in construction to the rest, yet it had an iron door and a sentry guard. The Phantom decided to investigate its need for a sentry. It was as good a place to start as any.

With Devil still faithfully following, he prowled through the shadows, got to the rear of the small, single-roomed house. The back wall was blank. The peaked roof was made of galvanized iron. A warning finger at Devil to stay quiet, a powerful heave of his arms, and he landed on the roof as lightly as a falling feather.

A two-man perimeter patrol found the tunnel under the fence, and the huge dog tracks in the sand. Under orders to report all unusual events, they immediately sent for General Serge. He cursed volubly on being awakened, yet got up and slid into civilian clothes immediately. This missile site on the Island of Dogs was his responsibility and his alone—until the official takeover next week. Despite a crushing schedule of eighteen hours per day, he demanded he be called for anything unusual.

He was a bear of a man, big, long-armed, thick-legged, broad-shouldered, thick graying blond hair cropped close. His blue eyes were red-rimmed, he had huge bags under them, his long face was falling into even longer lines of fatigue, yet he drove himself on. He lit one of the six-inch-long Slavic cigarettes he smoked incessantly, coughing at the first inhalation. Not even three inches of cotton packing in the butt end of the cigarette could cut the harshness of Mahorka tobacco, but he was used to this powerful rustic tobacco and thought Western cigarettes effeminate.

The perimeter patrol stiffened to attention when they saw him. General Serge was as tough a commander as they had ever had, a real slave driver who expected more from a man than he had to give. Still, his underlings had to admit he worked harder than anyone else on the island, and they were proud of his toughness. It would be something to talk about during the loneliness of the steppe camps. When your comrades complained about what a martinet the present commander was, you could reach back in your memory for General Serge and tell them what it was like to be under a really tough commander.

General Serge snapped his fingers to remind them they were in civilian clothes, and they relaxed—almost. One of the sentries shone a light on the tunnel and the tracks. Both of them waited. You never knew how the General was going to react.

"You woke me for that?" he growled.

"Sir," one of the sentries hastened to explain. "Those dog tracks—bigger than any dog tracks I ever saw. There aren't supposed to be any dogs on the Island of Dogs."

"Thickhead! Is it so impossible for an animal to swim from the mainland?"

The sentry thought of mentioning the length of the swim, the swift currents, the sharks, and decided he'd rather try to swim to the mainland than argue with General Serge. He stayed quiet.

The other sentry said, "General, there is a disturbing element here. Could a large dog tunnel under the fence without touching it? We should have here an animal corpse, not footprints."

There was something to the argument, and the General made a concession. "Then set a trap, you fool."

He lumbered away, puffing on his cigarette. Fatigue was wasting him like a disease. He could hold on for another week, he knew that, he was still clearheaded, a few hours' sleep while waiting for the relief was all he needed. Afterwards, it would be a long vacation in the Land of Roses and then . . . then . . .

He had been a raw recruit at the outbreak of the Great Patriotic War, called up with his age group and thrown at the advancing tanks to stop them with their bodies. They hadn't stopped them but they had delayed them, and the time they had bought with their blood was invaluable. Serge had fought and stepped back and fought and stepped back till the entire year had the quality of a nightmare, and he found himself a sergeant commanding troops he didn't know. The troops died, and there were more. He became a lieutenant and, at last, in six months of fire and death and explosion and summer heat and freezing cold, they stopped the tanks in a battle that became an epic.

Then it was their turn to attack. Serge had been ferried across a strait to reinforce troops who had gone there one night and died the next morning. The Little Land, they called it, an unsung battle to the rest of the world, but his country knew who had fought there and what they had done there. Serge had officially been acclaimed a hero, promoted to captain, and received the final honor of being made a member of the Party.

Not bad for a peasant's son. A captain. He had been severely wounded shortly afterwards, and on recovery commanded troops invading the lair of the enemy. He was in the spearhead of the honored army that fought its way into the enemy's capital. By then all knew that only the merciless survived, he who threw the first grenade and fired the quickest shots lived, and thereafter they attacked over a carpet of enemy bodies. He drove his men day and night and for his efforts was raised to the rank of major.

Major! He had started as an ant and ended as an eagle. He had immense power and undreamed of luxuries. Foods such as he had never known. He who had obeyed everyone's orders now gave them. It was a position worth scheming for, and Serge knew his own failings better than his records showed.

He had received compulsory education and won the right

to go on to higher education, but the war had stopped that before it started. Therefore he went to his old generals who knew him as a good fighting man, and asked to be sent to the military academy. They gave him letters of recommendation, and after intensive testing, and after approval by the political branch, he was granted admission.

This academy wasn't for cannon-fodder youths who showed some promise. This was the higher academy, which was expected to turn out the material that makes generals. Only members of the Party gained entrance here, and as Serge was acutely aware his membership was honorary, not earned in the political arena, he became a political activist. Not too outstanding, not a theorist who might spout the wrong theory and lose his head for it, but a good solid worker. If something needed doing, Serge did it. If someone was needed to give a speech, he volunteered, checked his written copy with the official books of the Party, and at the last asked his political superiors to check it for accuracy. He didn't take chances. He wasn't going back to toil on a farm or in a labor camp for committing political heresy.

He made it by hard work and unremitting effort. After that his rise was slow, steady, and unspectacular. He stayed in the shadows because the Great Father looked with distrust on shining ambitious young men, who sometimes had fatal "accidents" or simply disappeared, never to be heard from again.

Leadership changed and changed again, and the Leader became the one who had been the head of politics in the Little Land. General Serge—he wore two stars but he was only the equivalent of a brigadier general in the West— thought he could use this to his advantage; it was time for him to come out of the shadows, perform something brilliantly spectacular, take his seat on one of the thrones of power.

He went about it in his usual way, researching, studying, documenting, accumulating vast amounts of notes, sifting through them till only precious knowledge was left. Two years it took him, and he didn't consider a minute of that time wasted. Another month was spent preparing his plan, then he typed it and sent it to the Leader, and sat back to wait for the summons.

It never came. An autumn and a winter came, but not the summons to the capital. Desperate now, and believing the Leader had never seen his report, he took a leave, traveled to the capital, went straight from the airport to the Fortress of Power.

His rank got him through the gates, but then was made to wait in an office full of supplicants. Days passed, secretaries sidetracked him, he sat among the mighty and the powerful and they got no further than he did. Only those summoned entered the doors.

General Serge, therefore, resorted to his usual method. He

schemed. He impressed one of the soldier-secretaries with what he could do for him, elicited the bureaucrat's promise to deliver a simple message to the Leader:

I respectfully request an audience on a matter I believe is of importance to our beloved country. From one who fought with you in the Little Land.

General Serge

It was a miracle. It was the key that opened the doors. The Leader had been wounded in the Little Land and would refuse nothing to the few survivors. Perhaps he thought he could give this general another medal and send him on his way, or change his assignment for him, do him some sort of favor in commemoration of the shattering experience they, had shared—and then get rid of him.

But General Serge, after saluting the Leader, sat down and outlined an ambitious plan—ambitious, for he was an ambitious man who aspired to the stars, the stars of a Colonel, General or a Field Marshal. It was a plan like an ax, mostly naked power, but because the ax would be hidden till it was sharp there was also a certain subtlety to it. The Leader appreciated the political astuteness shown; the neighbors on the Eastern border were most troublesome, and bolstering there left the Western borders stripped, a thought that shivered the spine, for the enemy that had nearly destroyed them in the Great Patriotic War was a power again. Now the mushroom cloud would threaten all equally.

General Serge was put up in luxury while the Leader thought about the plan and talked about it to those who had pushed themselves to power through shrewdness and ruthlessness. After much discussion and weighing, the Leader gave his answer.

General Serge would get all the men and equipment he needed to convert this deserted island to a missile base. If he was caught by one of the great nations while constructing the site, the Leader would disown him, say he was in rebellion, was a traitor to his own country, and he'd suffer the consequences. If he succeeded, his reward would be commensurate with the risk. The choice was his.

Eagerly, Serge accepted. He had confidence in his own abilities.

Preparations alone took him two years; however, the careful detailing of his plan was worth the expenditure of time. One week away from success. The thought didn't drive away the fatigue, yet a certain amount of elation did seep through the overwhelming covering of weariness. Now, near the end, was no time to let down. He had to drive harder, get everything ready for the troops and technicians and scientists who'd come pouring in, make the island impregnable to attack. Or, too dangerous to attack.

He was passing the tool-shed which had been converted into a detention cell, lighting one Mahorka from another, when he heard the voice of the prisoner shouting in English, "Let me out of here. Serge! I demand to see you."

The sentry jerked open the iron door, ran inside, slammed his rifle butt into the stomach of the prisoner. He came out again, slamming and locking the door behind himself, ignoring the moans from inside.

General Serge had observed the entire scene. "Moron!" he bellowed. "I told you no violence with him."

"But, General," the guard tried to explain, "he was yelling."

"Let him yell. Who can hear him?" Serge was still furious. "And I've told you a thousand times, you cretin, that when I'm in civilian clothes I'm to be addressed as a civilian. Is that so hard, you camel's head? And you stand there in front of the door like a vegetable. Make yourself useful, you dolt. Walk around like you had something to do, you stinking fish. Get on sentry beat, you miserable mistake for a human."

The sentry trotted off, glad to get away from the General's wrath. Serge muttered to himself, angry at the stupidity of the soldiery he had chosen. Didn't they have any brains? Didn't they have any initiative? Must he watch over them as though they were babies and guide their every act? It wasn't like that during the Great Patriotic War. Men were men then. They stood up and died like heroes.

He lumbered off to his quarters, anxious to return to bed. He needed whatever sleep he could get.

Who can hear him, General Serge had asked, referring to the prisoner. One more person had.

The Phantom!

He was on the reverse slope of the roof, listening, hearing everything.

As Serge's footsteps retreated, the Phantom came down off the roof, landing lightly, and peered through the small window in the toolshed.

The prisoner was sitting on a bunk, holding his head and his stomach. He was elderly yet appeared vigorous, with the remnants of blazing good looks. His features were strong with a certain hawkish cast. Of medium height, he was deep-chested, broad-shouldered, and even bent over as he was now, you could see he would hold himself erect under other circumstances. The eyebrows were jet black, while the full head of white hair flowed long and his sideburns grew down thickly to join a luxurious moustache.

He raised his head. Matthew Helm. The missing Major Matthew Helm. He was being held here as a prisoner. It was to this place that he disappeared.

The Phantom prepared himself for action.

Janice Helm navigated the wave-cut channel with skill, letting the sea push the bow of the motorboat up onto the beach of the little cove.

"Here we are," she said brightly, jumping onto the sand. "Said I'd get us here."

"Shhh!" Riggs warned. "This place is dangerous."

"Nonsense. Granddaddy owns the island."

"You should have told that to the anti-aircraft gunners before they shot at me. I don't think we should be here. We'd better go back while we can."

"Speak for yourself, John. Take the boat if you want. Onward and forward is my motto."

"Janice, the Jungle Patrol doesn't have jurisdiction here."

"Oh, explain that to a judge, not to me."

"But if we get in trouble we're on our own."

Janice thought of the Phantom. Man, did she want to be rescued by him. What a hunk of humanity. And this cop was in her way. "Look, pal," she explained, "I've tried to tell you that I'm used to trouble, and I'm used to being on my own. I know these facts assault your delicate ears, but that's the way it is. You want to go back, you go ahead, I won't even try to stop you."

Riggs's face was starched in determination. "Orders are to bodyguard you and that's what I'll do. Okay, let's go. Up these rocks here."

"Not in my high heels, I'm not. We'll stroll along the beach and see what we see."

They had no sooner come to the beach when they saw the tunnel under the fence.

"Well, look here," Janice cried gleefully, thinking of the Phantom. "Somebody knew I was coming."

"They might be expecting us," Riggs reasoned. "Picked us up on radar or detected us with sonar. I feel too much like the fly being invited into the spider's kitchen."

"John," Janice shook her blond hair, "you must lead a miserable life. You worry so much. Isn't it just barely possible somebody came here before us?"

"Well . . . yes. But I don't know Who."

"I do," she moved suddenly, and with a wiggle was under the fence and standing on the other side.

"C'mon, bodyguard, don't lose me now."

Much more deliberately, Riggs slid under. Placing his hands well in front of him, he pulled himself forward so his legs were sure not to touch the fence.

"Swell," Janice congratulated him. "Now let's go."

She turned, took one step, and fell flat on her face.

"Oof!" The breath was knocked out of her. She looked back reproachfully at her ankle buried in the sand. "Something held me," she complained.

"I'll—" Riggs made a sudden motion to help, but found he couldn't pull his right wrist away.

"Don't move," he warned, brushing only the top layer of sand. Under a film of grains, he saw a gleam of fine wire.

"It's tanglefoot wire," he licked his lips nervously. "You pull against it and it just gets tighter." With slow careful movements he started loosening the wire grasping his wrist. The idea was not to exert any strength at all.

Sweat was beading his upper lip. He spoke his fears aloud. "I hope we haven't set off an alarm."

In the communications room at the island, a red light on a makeshift board blinked furiously. The radioman pulled over his microphone, punched a switch.

"Perimeter Patrol One. Perimeter Patrol One. I have a red alert from the tunnel. Repeat. I have a red alert from the tunnel. Over."

One of the sentries near the fence line pulled his portable radio from a holster, clicked it to life. "Central Control, this is Perimeter Patrol One. Proceeding to tunnel at all possible speed. Please notify Duty Officer. Over."

"Message received, will comply with request. Over and out."

Private John Riggs withdrew his wrist. There were red lines where the tanglefoot had grabbed him. Too much struggling and arteries would have been severed. It was nasty stuff to use and, he thought, indicative of the compassion quotient of these so-called seafood packers.

He turned to work on Janice's foot. She had tightened it pretty badly with her first step, although the wire hadn't broken the skin. The basic problem was that a foot just wasn't as supple as a hand. However, one compensating factor was that he could use both his hands and instruct her to hold wires while he loosened them. He made rapid progress.

"Try it now."

She withdrew her foot, toe pointing down.

"Hold it!" he warned.

"Still catching?" she asked.

"Yes. Balance against me. Just one wire . . . that's it, you can put your shoe on now."

A strange voice said, "Can we help?"

Riggs and Janice looked up in surprise. The two guards were grinning, and the muzzles of their assault rifles pointed directly at them. One made a gesture with his thumb. "Move."

The other was still grinning. "Not a bad trap. Look at the pretty fish we caught."

Janice was indignant, probably more angry at herself for being scared than at the men for pointing rifles at her. "Listen you," she warned, "my grandfather owns this island and you're in plenty of trouble."

Riggs spoke calmly, "I don't think you impressed them."

"Correct," one of the sentries stated. "Get your hands up and march."

Janice noticed the expression on the guard's face. He was through joking. His heavy-handed sense of humor had dissipated. Now he was deadly serious and would shoot if provoked.

She marched.

The Phantom rapped on the window to attract Major Helm's attention. The Major was instantly alert, left the bunk, peered through the glass pane. The light at his back prevented him from seeing anything. Even when he used his hands as eyeshades he could make out only the outline of a face, and the lower half of a face at that

"Major Helm," the Phantom called. "I'm here to help you. Can you open the door from the inside?"

"No. It's locked. Who are you?"

"Explanations later." The Phantom tested the door latch. "This lock is weak."

"That door is made of iron. It won't give."

"The old story of one weak link in the chain. Turn off your light"

"That can be done only from the powerhouse. It's protected behind a wire shield."

"Lie your shoe heel on it."

Helm was impressed with how quickly the man's mind worked. A problem, an immediate answer. Helm slipped off his shoe. A few seconds' pause, then the sounds of hammering and finally the light went off. The Phantom had utilized the time to further test the door. It was iron, true enough, but it was set in wood. A foolishness. Like putting bulletproof glass in a cardboard house.

"Helm," his deep voice was soft yet carried clearly. "Stand to one side."

The Phantom tensed his muscles. It was an action similar to putting a fuse in a box of dynamite. Measuring the distance to the door, he planted his powerful legs on the floor, then drove forward, shoulder first, a human battering ram.

The iron door exploded out of its frame. Wood ripped and splintered. Screws tore loose. Hinges flew. The lock snapped in two distinct pieces.

Behind the hail of debris that shrapneled across the room, the door fell flatly, like a beaver's tail smacking water. The Phantom, still driving forward, regained balance in a single stride, and did a jump-turn to face the empty doorway.

Major Helm was shocked, couldn't quite believe what he had witnessed with his own eyes. He stuttered:

"Wh—Who are . . . what are you?"

"Quiet," the Phantom commanded. "The guard must have heard the noise."

Running feet pounded on the packed earth outside. The guard braked when he saw the detention cell was dark, took a flashlight off his belt, held it in one hand and his rifle in the other. He searched back and forth with the beam till he found Major Helm.

"How did this door get open?" He stepped inside to threaten the prisoner.

There was never time for an answer. Phantom took a step forward and swung a full-armed swing. When the fist landed, the guard's face was distorted from the impact, his body came completely off the floor, twisted in midair and crashed into a far corner.

The Phantom grabbed Helm by the arm. "Let's move. Major."

Matthew Helm was dragged along willingly, trying to keep pace with the strides of this extraordinary man. Even as he went, his curiosity overwhelmed him.

"I don't know you. Who sent you? Janice?"

"Introductions later. I found a cave up in the rocks that will be a good hiding place. Can you make it?"

"Yes, I know the spot. But that guard will report—"

"No, he'll sleep till dawn."

Only then did Helm notice the giant mountain wolf pacing in front of them, a sort of advance guard, and his bewilderment increased. The masked man utilized the shadows but otherwise took little trouble at concealment, relying on the ears and nose of this ferocious "pet" to give him warning. Helm kept wondering what kind of a man wore such an esoteric costume, was masked, could break down iron doors, knock a man unconscious for hours, master a wolf so completely—the animal was obviously fond of him, gladly obeyed him—and that was love, not fear.

When they came to the rocks, the masked man took his arm in a steel grip, helping him in such a fashion that he was lucky his feet touched the ground. If ever there was a sensation of flying, this was it. Yet he sensed the man was trying to be gentle while hurrying. This implication of restrained power did more to build Helm's trust in the stranger than did the actual escape.

The cave was hidden behind a shield of rock that was like a building wall jutting out of the earth. The cave mouth was only some three feet high, although the interior of the recess was higher and wider. Helm scrambled in, sat down, attempted to catch his breath— and his wits.

The masked man stood by him. "Now then," his deep voice had an accusatory tone to it, "those nuclear warhead rockets down there bear the insignia of a Euro-Asian nation. Why did you lease this island to them as a missile base?"

"I didn't," Matthew Helm protested. "I thought I was leasing it to seafood packers. Would I have been held prisoner if I was aiding them?"

"It could be a falling-out between partners. I'll listen to your story. Start at the beginning."

"Yes, that would be best. The Helm family is an old family–"

"You don't have to go back that far," Phantom interrupted. There was still much he had to do.

"I have to," Helm insisted. "It's the only way of explaining so you'll understand my ancestors and understand me. The Helms, you may know, were a reckless and adventurous lot."

"I've read history."

"Yes, they wrote history. They were exploring strange places before the explorers did. They were empire-builders, and they carved out empires for themselves. Most of them became fabulously wealthy. But the same characteristics that earned them every material possession also ruined them. Those lusty forebears of mine couldn't stand peace. I mentioned they were reckless, didn't I? They squandered fortunes on wine, women and song, but it was always gambling that ruined them. All of them. All of us. Compulsive gambling. Richard Helm, for one, lost a country on the turn of a card. Howard Helm lost a fleet of merchant ships. I could go back three hundred years telling you of their exploits and ultimate ruin. The one saving grace all of us had was that we recognized this flaw in ourselves, and therefore, when we were rich, we put aside a little bit—a pittance— for the next generation, enough for an education and a start. That's all the old Helms ever needed—a start. Then each soared to the sun and fell broken to the sea. I, myself, lost a villa and farm, a textile mill, and an oil field. Yes, I owned an entire oil field..." His eyes glazed in reverie.

"Island of Dogs," the Phantom prompted.

Matthew Helm shrugged. "The least of our possessions. Couldn't sell it, and it wasn't worth anything as a gambling stake else it would have been out of the family long ago. We owned it outright, but who wants a waterless desert island that's only a menace to navigation? Well, I put aside enough in a trust fund I couldn't touch for Janice, my granddaughter, and—oh, three years ago, found myself flat broke. Sufficient to exist and that was all. I was ending like all the Helms. I felt my life was over.

"Then two years ago, my lawyer, Lionel Crabbe, introduced me to an executive of a worldwide seafood packing company. At least that's what Crabbe said he was. Serge, the executive, said he wanted to buy Dog Island so his firm could develop a secret packing process. Outside of the house in Mawitaan, it was the last thing the last Helm possessed. I asked myself what he would pay for a worthless desert island? Enough to make me more aware of my poverty, and that was all. For those reasons—and to hide my shame—I told him no. It was the last vestige of my foolish pride asserting itself."

Helm sighed. "I thought that was the end of it. But a few weeks later, Crabbe and Serge were back with a hundred-year lease at a fantastic annual rental, fifty years' rent in advance, and payment would be in gold. I tell you I thought a miracle had happened. I never had a thought as to why the island was suddenly valuable, or why this outrageous sum in advance. My only fear was that Serge would realize he was insane and revoke his offer. I signed before he could get away."

Major Helm smiled ironically. "You can imagine what happened. Monte Carlo, Deauville, Biarritz, Las Vegas, Rio, London, Hong Kong, Singapore, the traditional path of the fatal Helm diseases: wine, women, song—and gambling. But ah, what a time! I was rejuvenated. I spent with both fists. I fixed up the Mawitaan place, sent Janice money, and spent, and spent, and spent. I returned here to Mawitaan, telling myself I wanted to see Janice and the progress on the island. Of course my real purpose, I realize now, was to attempt to get the other fifty years' rent."

He sighed heavily. "That was my first mistake—informing Crabbe I wanted to inspect the island. He said that under the terms of the lease it was impossible. I have been in business, you understand, and this outright lie irritated me. I slammed his desk and informed him in no uncertain terms I was going to inspect the Island of Dogs with or without his permission, and if necessary, I'd have an army of police at my back. Well, that was my second and last mistake. That same night, while Janice was away, two thugs broke in."

The Phantom nodded. "One with a moustache, the other like a walking brick."

"Yes, I can guess you met them. I hope you wrecked them thoroughly. They took me here blindfolded and at gunpoint. Serge was waiting for me with a new contract. I was to sign the island over to his country for whatever purposes they wished, and the price, sir, was astronomical. Of course, I ripped the papers up and had the great pleasure of throwing the pieces in his face."

"The Helms, Major, were always men."

"Thank you. A great compliment, especially coming from a man such as yourself. However, I suspect the truth was I feared I wouldn't live a second after signing the deed. Serge has great self-control. He could have killed me then, but he had me locked up and told me if I didn't come to my senses I'd be shot and thrown to the sharks. I believe my time was fast running out when you rescued me. Which I do appreciate, sir. Did Janice send you?"

"In a way. This Serge nearly has the base completed."

"Yes. And I heard that five thousand more men will come the moment he finishes. The island will become impregnable. I lost count of the number of missiles, even the types of missiles. From here the nuclear warheads can hit any target in Africa and Asia. The balance of power is tipped."

"So then," the Phantom straightened, "it will have to be tipped back."

Major Helm threw up his hands in a hopeless gesture. "What can you alone do against an army?"

"That's what I'll have to find out. I have till dawn. Stay here, Major, and be quiet."

The masked man left in lithe strides, the giant wolf at his heels. Matthew Helm shook his head. An impossible task. Impossible. Even for such an overwhelming man as this modern Hercules.

The Phantom had earlier noticed a squat building with a very thick roof and a wide overhang. The major portion of it seemed to be sunk in the ground. This was the typical construction of a munitions dump, and he would have investigated it before had not the nuclear rockets attracted his attention. Now he went to it and had easy access. The path leading to the door began some distance away at ground level, then went down gradually into the earth, forming a ditch at the entrance that was deeper than a man—even the Phantom—was tall.

The metal door—it wasn't steel or iron, probably some sort of an alloy—had Cyrillic characters written on it, and in English the command, "Keep Out—Authorized Personnel Only."

The Phantom didn't keep out. The door was secured only by a latch, as a munitions dump door should be. If a door is locked and an emergency occurs as emergencies do, then the key has to be obtained and the delay can lose a battle. In danger zones, a dump is well guarded against the possibility of capture or sabotage; however, General Serge, a cautious man, believed the sea, the electric fence, and a thousand personnel working around the dump were guard enough. And he would have been right in almost any other case.

The inside was a revelation. Not only were there rifles in racks and machine pistols in cases, all with masses of accompanying ammunition, plus shells for the mortars and anti-aircraft guns in nose-up readiness on the floor, but all the construction explosives such as dynamite and TNT were here, piled box on box. This was the best evidence of the frenzied haste made in building the missile base. In any other operation, weapons and explosives would have been stored separately.

The Phantom, like all brilliant men, took advantage of every opportunity given him. He paused in thought for a moment, making and discarding plans, then an idea burgeoned in his mind. It might work. It was risky, it was a case of win all or lose all, but it was the only Chance there was.

He started shifting cases to the locations he wanted, ran explosive cord on the floor to connect everything, and covered it with dirt. A box of dynamite was buried outside the door.

"Now," he said to Devil, "we need a timing mechanism. "And," he picked up two more cases of dynamite, "we'll leave tokens of our intentions on the way."

Deliberately he walked to the guardhouse as the place most likely to have an alarm clock, making two detours to bury his dynamite, wrapping explosive cord around each case, crimping a fuse on the end of the cord, then leaving the fuse sticking unobtrusively out of the ground. The way he planted the dynamite cases there was no danger of their being kicked or stepped on.

At the guardhouse, he peered through the window. It was as he guessed. These soldiers were no different from any other soldiers throughout the world. A civvy-clad man, probably a sergeant, was grabbing a snooze on a bunk while the privates walked their tour of duty. Beside him on a table was an alarm clock and a flashlight.

The Phantom opened the window and stepped in, all in one quiet movement. He pushed down the alarm button on the clock, hoping the click would wake the sergeant.

It did. His eyes snapped open. He started to struggle up. The Phantom's steel fist inscribed a short arc, crashed on the sergeant's jaw. The sergeant's head jerked, and he sprawled on the bunk, sleeping again. Besides the missing clock and flashlight, there was the Skull Mark on his chin to prove he had been visited.

In the munitions dump, the Phantom stripped insulation off electric wire, taped the batteries together, and wired the clock so it completed an electric circuit. Placing the clock in a hole he had dug, he placed a board over it, burying everything. One last look around to be sure there were no signs of his work. The floor appeared the same as when he had first entered.

"That's the first part of it," he told Devil. "The rest had better work as smoothly. Come on, boy, we have to fight a bear."

Major Helm was sitting behind the rock shielding the cave, watching the bowl below. The masked man had said the guard would sleep till dawn, but that was an awfully long time to be unconscious and a prudent man didn't take chances. Another fear was that Serge's men knew of the presence of the cave. They had been on the island quite a while and could have done some exploring. Therefore, if they discovered his escape, this was one of the first places they'd look, and he didn't want to be trapped. He could dodge around these rocks to prevent discovery, and there was always the hope of somehow getting off the island.

Janice Helm and Private Riggs were being marched by the sentries to headquarters, hands over head. Matthew Helm watched the little procession several seconds before he understood what was happening. Impulsively he yelled, "Janice!"

She whirled around. "Granddad?"

Both guards leaped back in the "on guard" position. One was quick-witted, grasped the situation, shouted, "Come down out of there or I'll shoot both of them."

Major Helm put up his hands and picked his way through the rocks. He couldn't risk Janice's life, and he was well aware these soldiers were ruthless. When he reached the party, he said, "I'm sorry, my dear. Shouldn't have given myself away like that. What are you doing here?"

"Oh, Granddad," her voice was sorrowful, "I was looking for . . . What are you doing here?" She was suddenly surprised at seeing him. "I thought you were in Europe."

"No. I'm a captive. Like you. That Serge!" he raged, thinking Janice had been kidnapped.

"Shut up!" was the harsh command from the sentry. "All of you. Move on!"

The dreary group slowly walked towards headquarters, and to what Major Helm sincerely believed was the last confrontation with General Serge.

CHAPTER 10

Serge's aide, a burly lieutenant, burst into the General's room without knocking. Serge, opening his eyes, didn't bother to rise. Perhaps he could solve the problem without getting up.

"Sorry to disturb you, sir," the aide began, "but Major Helm escaped. We just recaptured him."

"Then why bother me," Serge growled. "Stuff him back in the shed and chain him to something." He closed his eyes, already plummeting into sleep.

"And the trap we set was sprung by two more coming under the fence."

Serge threw off the covers, sat up, roared, "What is this island turning into? The Leipzig Fair? Are we a convention center?"

Because of the constant disturbances, he wore his trousers to bed, and therefore could jump directly into his boots. "Doesn't our radar work? Or are our technicians fast asleep? Who are these people?"

"The man is from the Jungle Patrol."

"What! Is he a scout for an invasion?"

"Not likely, General. When Gregoire and Nicholas failed for whatever reason outside that absurd story they told us, this Patrolman was assigned to the girl as—"

Serge spun around, shouting, "The girl is Janice Helm?"

"Yes, sir. We found her boat in a cove we didn't know existed. It's her personal boat, not a Jungle Patrol boat. Therefore we can draw the conclusion . . ." the aide's voice petered out when he saw he had lost the General.

Serge lit a Mahorka, blowing smoke thoughtfully. "Well, well," he mused. "The capture of the granddaughter has genuine possibilities." Acting with deliberation to give himself more time to think, he took his military tunic off a hook, slipped it over his heavy shoulders, buttoned it completely, even to the choker collar. Another puff on the Mahorka, an exhalation, a nod.

"Alright. I'll see the prisoners now."

The aide led the way to the office, slipping his machine pistol off his shoulder and holding it at the ready.

The office was spartan. Serge hadn't wasted effort on amenities. A desk with phones atop it, working lights, and a wall lined with filing cabinets were all he needed.

Serge stood at the door and stared at the three prisoners. "So," he commented. "I catch one and two follow. How many more can I expect?"

Whenever Janice Helm was caught in trouble, she brazened it out. Now she spoke in tones of bravado. "You're the first seafood packer in military uniform I ever saw."

Serge's eyes shifted to her. "A sharp tongue and a pretty face. A bad combination."

"Flattery gets you nowhere. You're in trouble, buster. Let us go now, and I'll be a character witness for you."

Serge snorted in amusement and was about to reply when a knock sounded on the door. "Come," he gave permission. An orderly stuck his head in.

"General, the sergeant of the guard was struck, and also reports his alarm clock and flashlight were stolen."

Serge whirled and threw his Mahorka stub at the orderly, shouting, "Get out of here with that nonsense. A week's punishment for the sergeant as an inducement to keep awake. And don't disturb me again. I'm conducting a court-martial."

"Court-martial!" Riggs howled, his legal mind objecting. "We're not military. We've done nothing to be brought before a court."

Serge motioned his aide aside, seated himself behind his desk, lit another Mahorka. "So you all understand," he exhaled. "Fact: this is occupied territory. Fact: this territory is under military control. Fact: you insinuated yourselves clandestinely into this territory. You are charged with being spies and are on trial for your lives."

"Our lives?" Riggs was still shouting mad. "It's ridiculous. I'm Miss Helm's bodyguard, and Major Helm here owns the island."

Serge's face was merciless. "Your statements will be taken later. The trial begins."

Major Helm held out his hand. "Serge, I'll sign the deed."

The General's eyes merely flickered over him. "I don't need it now."

"Nevertheless, let these young people go, Serge. I beg of you. They have their whole lives in front of them."

"They should have considered that before coming here."

"Wait!" Rigg's mind was working at top speed. "There can't be a trial. There is no President of the Court. There is no Legal Officer. There is no Court to hear the evidence."

Serge's face was deadly. "My legalistic friend, I can do what I want. This is a Revolutionary Tribunal. I am the judge, the jury, and the prosecutor."

"Then they will need a defense attorney," the Phantom stepped through an open window, an automatic in his right hand. He had reached headquarters just in time to hear the General's last statement, and instantly decided this was the proper time to take charge.

His entrance caused something of a sensation.

Serge jerked his head around and said, "What?"

Major Helm breathed relief, "You."

Janice Helm exclaimed. "About time!"

The lieutenant guarding the prisoner saw the gun in the Phantom's hand and tried to get his machine pistol around.

He was a little late. Riggs, despite his arguing, was watching for any opening, and the moment the muzzle of the machine pistol turned away from him, he reacted with the instinct of long training. His left hand speared into the aide's stomach and as the lieutenant doubled over, wind knocked out of him, Riggs came down with a judo chop on the back of his neck. A jerk and a twist, and Private Riggs had the machine pistol. He pointed it at Serge.

Devil leaped through the window, licked his fangs and stood over the unconscious man.

The Phantom's deep voice filled the office. "Nice piece of work, Riggs. Keep the General amused."

Janice smiled brightly at the Phantom. "I knew I'd find you. What took you so long getting here?"

The Ghost Who Walks had no congratulations for her. "You're as foolish a child as I've ever met," he reprimanded. "I suspect if it weren't for Private Riggs you would have been dead long ago. Now get over there," he pointed to a blank wall, "stay out of harm's way, and keep quiet." His voice had the ring of command.

"Oh!" her hand flew to her mouth, and she bit down on one finger, tears starting in her eyes.

"And stop crying," he snapped. "The act is outdated."

He was mean. Cruel. Abominable. Loathsome. She didn't like him as much as she used to.

"Move!" his finger stabbed at the wall, and she skittered over. Major Helm chuckled. "Bully. Absolutely bully."

The byplay between Phantom and Janice had allowed General Serge to recover his wits and his nerve. He was surrounded by a thousand of his picked troops, he belatedly realized. What was there to worry about?

Serge's chuckle joined the Major's. "What's this, a masquerade. Who are you?"

"I told you I was the defense attorney. That was true at the time. The situation has changed in the last few seconds. I am your judge."

"Another lawyer?" Serge wondered, still amused.

"No. I'm a man who stole an alarm clock."

"What kind of crazy talk is that?" Serge threw his Mahorka into a large ashtray. With two guns pointing at him, he was getting irritated. It was time to end this charade. He started moving his hand under his desk.

"You might as well drop your guns. You are surrounded by my soldiers. They will come pouring in here a second after I press this alarm button."

"And a second after I press this trigger," Phantom held his automatic steadily and stared at Serge. "Do we understand each other, General?"

"Yes," Serge put his hands on top of the desk, took another Mahorka, lit it. "But do not think," he waved away the smoke cloud, "that I will not sacrifice my life if the price warrants it I remind you, all of you are still my prisoners; however, I recognize you have bargaining powers. You in that outlandish costume—you want something. I will negotiate. What is it?"

The Phantom's voice was cool and level. "I want you and your men to get off this island. At once!"

Serge roared laughter, pounded both fists on the desk, rocked back and forth in his swivel chair. "Ha, ha, ha, that is good. That is good. That is excellent. You have a big sense of humor," he controlled his laughter, wiped at his eyes.

"But that is not bargaining," he shook his head. "You think because you point two guns at me I will be scared and run away? Come now, be sensible. I'm not leaving this island and neither are you. Now what do you want?"

"I want you to leave this island peacefully."

Serge laughed again but it was controlled laughter. "I thought you would ask for your lives. I was willing to give you that. I am in such good humor. Tell me why I have to leave this island?"

The Phantom's penetrating voice never raised. "You are here illegally. You said you wished to build a seafood plant, instead you built a missile base. You have defrauded Major Helm."

"Ha!" Serge slapped the desk with his open palm. "Now you compare me to a tenant who makes too much noise, and you want to evict me. You are very funny."

"You won't find me amusing for long," the Phantom promised.

"No? Listen, comedian, all the nations in the United Nations couldn't force me off here. As for legality, I throw another fifty years' rent to that capitalist pig over there," he waved at Major Helm, "and he'll sign anything. A new lease, a deed to the island, ownership. Anything."

Major Helm spoke quietly, "No, Serge. Never again.'"

"Yes!" Serge shouted, enjoying himself. "I have what you; value most. Your granddaughter."

The Phantom's voice grew steely. "You would use force to stay on this island?"

"Of course. What can you do about it?"

"The same. I will use force to get you off."

"The joke goes too far. Do you think those guns are a threat to me? You must recognize by the medals on my tunic," his fingers flicked at his chest, "that I am willing to die for my country."

"Are you willing to sacrifice all your men—and still lose the base?"

"Oh goodness," Serge grew sarcastic. "Now I am scared. Do I have time to pack?"

"No!" the Phantom was as definite as the fall of the guillotine. "None of your men do, either. This base, everything on it, all the people, will be destroyed in exactly one hour and fifty minutes."

Serge saw the masked man was serious. "What!" He half rose out of the chair, then sat down again, thinking furiously. A threat to the base. How could that have happened? The answer was it couldn't. The island was perfectly protected. These few people had sneaked on shore at the one spot where they couldn't be detected, yet his patrols and traps had captured them. As for this masked man—

The General snapped to his senses. Whoever, he asked himself, had ever seen a man in such a ridiculous costume? Only a lunatic on parade would wear it. He must have escaped from an asylum. Trust a loony to have made it to the island. Of course he was armed, and a madman with a gun was dangerous—

The Phantom shared his train of thought. "General, you are now thinking I'm mad; I can't carry out my threat. Correct?"

Serge swallowed hard. The statement was psychologically devastating. Was he a mind reader? Could a madman follow such an involved line of thought such as he, the General, had been pursuing? On second thought, that costume looked more menacing than comical. And the automatic was very, very real. The steadiness of the hand holding the weapon, it was incredible under these circumstances. Only now did Serge realize that under his tunic he was sweating profusely. He, a combat veteran of two wars. He who had stood in hell and fought off the enemy. A hero of the nation, and he was sweating with fear.

The Phantom said, "One hour and forty-five minutes. You'll need time to board the boat and get clear of the island. Go!"

"Leave?" Serge's anger exploded. "The gun doesn't frighten me. Shoot!" he threw his arms wide and waited.

The Phantom remained calm. "That's too easy, General. It's what you want. Then you won't have to make a decision, and decisions of this magnitude always warp the mind. I'll help you reach that decision. It was reported to you an alarm clock was stolen, correct?"

Serge thought back. It seemed so long ago. "Yes, yes," he nodded.

"I'm counting time, General. What are alarm clocks used for? On a base where there are large quantities of munitions and explosives? One hour and forty-three minutes. A flashlight was also stolen. What are batteries used for? An alarm clock and batteries."

"A timing device," Serge gasped. "For a time bomb."

"Correct. One hour and forty-two minutes."

Serge tried to light a cigarette with trembling fingers. The flame and the cigarette finally passed each other often enough to light the Mahorka. He took a deep breath, trying to regain control of himself. Think! Think! He had been in tight places before.

All right, an alarm clock was stolen, that was a fact.

Wait a minute! Was a fact necessarily evidence? A missing alarm clock didn't equate with a time bomb. The masked man could have been listening outside the window, heard the report about the alarm clock, concocted this whole scheme on a stupidly misplaced clock. There was one way to test the theory.

He sat back in his swivel chair, puffed the Mahorka. How calm he was now; how steady his nerves. He was hardly sweating. He put on an attitude of nonchalance, said, "We seem to have reached an impasse. Either way, it seems I die. I'm willing to wait till the whole island blows up."

"I'm not, General. The island will explode, but I want these people safely away before then. It's true you will die before I leave here. I came here unseen, and I can leave unseen, so don't depend on your men. The regret I have is that they will die too. Needlessly. One hour thirty-five minutes. Your move, General."

Serge shook his head. "As you say, clown, it's my move. I hope you play chess. Do you think I'm going to be caught in a fool's mate? Two moves and out? I won't make any moves. I'll sit here. You shoot me and the orderly outside hears the shot."

The Phantom made a counter move. "He rushes in here and Riggs shoots him."

"The rattle of a machine pistol is heard outside. Men come to investigate."

"We're gone by then. And they still don't know a time bomb has been planted."

"Obviously, the orderly hasn't murdered me, the prisoners have. The island is secured by a thousand men. You're handicapped by the girl and are discovered."

"I'm the only one who knows where the bomb is. Do you think they could make me talk?"

Serge smiled, revealing his gap teeth. "And all this is based on the supposition there is a bomb."

"You're right," the Phantom agreed. "Are there any explosives on this island outside the munitions dump?"

"No. None."

"Watch," the Phantom raised his automatic. "The last flatcar on the end of the tracks."

"No!" Serge jumped. "Nuclear warhead."

The automatic glided to eye level, stopped rock-steady. The Phantom's fist had been squeezing all the while and the same instant the weapon paused, it fired.

The flatcar leaped up atop a growing flower of flame. The trucks came off, an axle broke, and iron wheels scaled. The car kept rising on the expanding explosion, looking much like an awkward, rocket. The bed broke in two as the car reached the summit of its rise, and the train pieces started to descend. But the load it had carried was still gaining altitude. One short-range rocket whirled around like a helicopter blade. The other arrowed high and arched down to the ground, where it crashed.

The sound was momentarily deafening, literally. The concussion wave was a destroying hand. The glass was knocked out of the office windows. Concrete dust rained down on them.

In the barracks men were tumbled out of their beds. On a tower, two workmen standing on a beam a foot off the ground were lifted off it and seated on a beam five feet higher. Generators overturned and welding machines stopped. Trucks had windshields shattered. Cranes swayed precariously, hooks swinging. The oceangoing freighter at the pier rolled.

"No nuclear warheads," the Phantom still stood at the window, unharmed. "I checked." Everyone was running towards the rail track. It was what he wanted. They were running away from the next danger.

"Now General," he announced. "Watch the near tower."

Again the muscle-knotted arm rose. Again the weapon fired. Again the hammer stroke of noise and concussion. Concrete dust filled the room.

"Stop it! Stop it!" Janice held her ears and screamed.

But her screams were erased by the shrieking of the tower, three-legged now as it leaned over. Kept tilting over, over. More and more of it smashed into the ground, and it looked something like a child's toy being destroyed with beams leaping out of the dust cloud in a crazy pattern.

The dust started to settle, but men ran in confusion. On the desk telephones jangled insistently. No one paid attention to them. They weren't important at this moment

The Phantom turned from the window. "One hour and twenty-eight minutes. Have I been at the munitions dump. General?"

"Yes," Serge whispered, then suddenly he cracked wide open, beat his fists against his head, howled like a wild dog.

"I can't fail! Do you understand that? I can't fail! I can't order evacuation. Kill me now!"

"Attention!" the Phantom's voice ship-cracked, and Serge went rigid. "Control yourself! Be at ease," his voice relented, and lapsed into soothingly reasonable tones.

"General, when you were in, combat, were you ever forced by military necessity to retreat?"

"Yes," Serge slumped in the chair, drenched in sweat, "in the beginning, the first two years, many times."

"General, I assure you this island will explode in one hour and twenty-four minutes. You are faced with superior force. There is nothing you can do about it. The island will be destroyed. Keep that in mind—the island will blow up. This is not a defeat. This is a strategic withdrawal to preserve the lives of your men."

The Phantom was very careful not to use the word "fail." In Serge's country, failure meant a fatal "accident" or a disappearance into a labor camp.

The Phantom went on, "You can bring your own men back to their native land. You had to leave because the island was about to be destroyed. It was heroic of you to save their lives."

"Yes," Serge looked at him, "but if they ever find out the 'superior' forces are a girl, a boy, an old man, and a costumed lunatic with a gun . . ."

The Phantom's voice became staccato as he urged the General, "You think those men out there won't back you to the limit? You're being bombed, Serge. The planes are chopping you to pieces. You don't know by whom, Serge. Perhaps planes from your own country. A general is trying to get even with you or overthrow your government. Your security men can take lie-detector tests, go under truth serum, and say without fear of refutation that no Western nation knows about the Island of Dogs. Who's doing it. Serge? Who's doing it?"

"I don't know," Serge shouted.

"No. It's a long voyage home. You'll try to find out Question troops. Send wires. Use the radio. Investigate. Keep investigating. Demand answers. Demand them from the Leader. Act now!"

Serge mopped sweat from his face. He looked up, and his question was a plea. "You're sure it'll work?"

The Phantom's retort bounced back. "It will! You have a thousand witnesses."

Serge grabbed microphone, inhaled to control himself. "This is General Serge speaking," he announced, and echoes bounced around the island. "This is General Serge. We are under attack. Repeat, we are under attack. All personnel will get to the ship at once. Do not pack. Leave your tools. Go to the ship. Stop what you're doing. Go to the ship at once. Let the fires burn, it doesn't matter anymore, get to the ship. Don't dress, don't stop for anything. Board the ship at once."

The Phantom reached over and clicked off the microphone. "That's enough to convince them. When they're aboard, you may leave."

Over the crackling of the fire started by the explosions came the sound of hurrying feet. The soldiers, in obedience to orders, were double-timing to the ship. Some were half-dressed. One had shaving cream on his jowls. Only a few carried weapons. They were ordered to take nothing, they went empty-handed. They were disciplined. There was one thing you could say about General Serge. He knew how to discipline men.

A loudspeaker announced from the ship, "All men aboard, General. Steam is up in the boilers. We are waiting for you."

The Phantom holstered his revolver. He had stood as steady as a carving all through the evacuation. Janice was inclined to believe he was four hundred years old. Private Riggs had recognized the Commander's voice, but was in the same quandary as Colonel Weeks—who was the Phantom? Matthew Helm wondered if any of the dare-devil Helms had been quite like this man, and was thankful he had lived to see a generation in which this man existed. Serge stood. He turned to the Phantom.

"Tell me. Would you have shot me?"

"Yes. You brought war here. You would have died here."

"And then the attempt at escape, huh?"

"I would have escaped. An hour and twelve minutes. Leave."

Serge paused at the door. He was quite recovered now. "Who are you working for?"

"Mankind. All men. Yours too."

Serge closed the door. The Phantom watched him walk to the ship, then quickly turned.

"Janice! Is your speedboat still here?"

"I think so. They didn't do anything to it."

"Quick then. A little less than an hour to make it."

Janice squawked, "You mean the island's actually going to blow up?"

Riggs grabbed her by the arm, rushed her out. "You think he was joking? Those two explosions were just warm-ups before the main event!"

They ran across the burning base. The fires were spreading to the discarded lumber piles. Damage looked extensive, yet an experienced eye could tell it was superficial.

At the rocks, the Phantom took the puffing Major Helm by the arm. Riggs was pushing Janice, although even he had to admit she was doing well by herself.

Approaching the fence, Riggs sprinted forward. He threw himself on his knees, sifted his fingers through the sand till he found the alarm wire. A tug on it and the tanglefoot sprang to the surface. Once seen, it could be pushed to one side.

The Phantom added a warning: "Careful. The fence is still electrified."

Major Helm gasped, "How much more time?"

"Forty-two minutes," the Phantom answered laconically. Janice wiggled under the fence. "You mean this is for real? A whole island is going to explode?"

The Phantom gave her a Delphic answer. "Lead the way to the boat. Take it out of here at full speed."

The motorboat was still nosed up on the beach. Riggs, Janice, and the Major piled in. The Phantom stooped, lifted the bow, gave a mighty heave, planed the boat out on the water. Devil seemed to bounce off the cove bottom, then was in the stern, shaking himself, wetting everyone. The Phantom made one of his soaring leaps, caught the side of the boat, lifted himself into the front seat. It was his sense of urgency that finally convinced Janice time was of the essence. The boat's prow jumped out of the water as she accelerated.

On the bridge of the steaming freighter, Serge looked back to the island. He had the feeling he had been caught in a dishonest poker game. Well, he thought, if the island does not explode in the time span given by the masked man, he'd send in the helicopter with guard troops for the munitions dump, launch the small boats to rush additional soldiers to strategic points. The island could be reoccupied in a half hour.

On the main deck, a vast majority of the soldiers and sailors were watching the island. They had been told nothing except that they were under attack, but they could make their own guesses, were comparing experiences, and counting themselves lucky to be alive. Rumors were going up one side of the ship and coming back in a different form down the other. Conjecture grew and grew. Pretty soon a large number of men were trying to describe the planes they had seen diving down and bombing them. One story was matched, then surpassed by the next.

Serge checked his watch. One second to go. Time!

And nothing happened. He had been bluffed. He had been suckered. He opened his mouth to issue the orders that would send occupying troops on their way.

A light grew in the sky, spread, till all the island was lit and could be distinctly seen. The light flickered, grew stronger till it seemed as though the sun were rising behind it

Then the island started to move. It was a ripple at first, a mere shrug. The surrounding sea shivered and turned white with foam. The very substance of the island shuddered, the light increased to flashbulb intensity, and parts of the island competed with each other in reaching for the sky.

The blast was cataclysmic. Pieces as large as an acre raced each other to the sky. The island was literally coming apart, was raining its substance upwards. The center of the explosion was a white-hot heat that seared the eyes, and the explosions on the fringe of heavy-caliber shells and cases of dynamite were very minor.

The sea rose in a wall as if standing back in horror, then it crashed in. The unearthly bright light went out. Now the sea boiled and was greatly disturbed by house-sized chunks pattering into it. Swirling, heaving, changed currents bucked each other and spewed water walls.

The noise was unimaginable. The minds of those viewing the explosion refused to let the individual they were encased in suffer and turned off hearing as a protective measure. But the heat wave could be felt as a roaring hot wind; minutes later there were minor bangs like the broadsides of battleships carrying sixteen-inch guns, and while the laws of physics state vibration and sound are distinct, each man on the freighter could feel what he heard.

Around the world seismograph needles soared and fell back down a staircase of their own making.

General Serge was shaking. Through binoculars, he saw the sea settle uneasily over a place where once had been an island. All that was left was a stretch of sand dune with a pile of rocks on one end.

He could have been there, he kept thinking. His pieces would have been scattered over miles—if that primordial explosion hadn't incinerated them altogether. Suddenly, he had a happy thought. At home there could be no doubting him now. Couldn't mention the masked man, though. The story was not only incredible; it was unfathomable. Have to start brainwashing the troops, tell them of their narrow escape. As if they didn't know already. He pulled the microphone close, making up a speech congratulating them on their coolness under attack.

At the Mawitaan estate of Major Helm, Janice asked the Phantom, "Would you really have sacrificed us in that explosion?"

"Janice," the Phantom's lip spread in amusement, "like Helen of Troy you are more valuable than a thousand ships and a thousand men. No one will ever convince you otherwise. I'm sure a way would have been found to spare you while the rest of us gave our all to the last."

"I think so too," she agreed seriously.

"Will you excuse me?" Major Helm asked. "I have to make phone calls to Chief of Police Togando and Colonel Weeks. That scoundrel lawyer of mine, Lionel Crabbe, misrepresented himself, mishandled my funds, acted as agent for a foreign power, and I'm sure an investigation will reveal further chicanery. It will be a pleasure putting him in jail."

The Phantom turned to Riggs and Janice. "I must go too. Take care of yourselves."

Janice grinned at him. "I'll be all right. I have a bodyguard."

Riggs called to the retreating figure, "Goodbye . . . Commander," but the Phantom didn't pause in his exit.

Later, Janice was showering the grime of adventure off, and Gooley was laying out fresh clothes.

The Llongo girl said, "Now you met the Ghost Who Walks, Miss Janice. Still in love with him?"

"Like being in love with lightning." Janice toweled vigorously. "Even if you do catch it, you're going to get yourself burned or killed. He's out of my league. I mean he's in a league of his own. How are you going to order around a man who scares off a thousand men at a time?"

She paused by the window, stared down at Riggs. "Now he's not bad. Not bad at all."

Coming Soon From Hermes Press

Volume 14: THE ASSASSINS